NUNSENSE

A Musical Comedy

Book, Music, and Lyrics by

Dan Goggin

WINNER
4 1986 OUTER CRITICS'
CIRCLE AWARDS
Including
BEST
OFF-BROADWAY
MUSICAL!

D1533988

SAMUEL FRENCH, INC.

45 WEST 25TH STREET   NEW YORK 10010
7623 SUNSET BOULEVARD   HOLLYWOOD 90046
LONDON   *TORONTO*

The Nun Puppet, the Cover for the "Baking with the B.V.M."
Cookbook, the "Dying Nun" Hat, the Slides for "Nunsmoke,"
authentic "Little Sisters of Hoboken Habits," the *Nunsense* Cast
Recording, and Nunsense Greeting Cards are available for
purchase from the Nunsense Theatrical Company, c/o Gatchell
and Neufeld, 165 West 46th Street, New York, NY 10036.

Cover art designed by Peter Gergely.

Dan Goggin came to New York from Alma, Michigan. He began his career as a singer in David Merrick's Broadway production of *Luther* starring Albert Finney. He then toured for five years as a member of the folksinging duo, "The Saxons." Dan wrote the music for and appeared in the off-Broadway musical *Hark!*, after which he began writing both music and lyrics for revues. He composed the score for the Broadway production *Legend* starring Elizabeth Ashley and F. Murray Abraham, and has written the book, music and lyrics for an original musical *A One-Way Ticket To Broadway*. *Nunsense* was first created by Dan Goggin and Marilyn Farina as a greeting card series. Based on the greeting card character, Dan wrote the "Nunsense" musical.

CHERRY LANE THEATRE

___

THE NUNSENSE THEATRICAL COMPANY

and

JOSEPH HOESL & BILL CROWDER

presents

NUNSENSE

A New Musical Comedy

Starring

(*in alphabetical order*)

CHRISTINE ANDERSON   VICKI BELMONTE

SEMINA DE LAURENTIS   MARILYN FARINA   SUZI WINSON

Written and Directed by
DAN GOGGIN

Musical Staging/Choreography by
FELTON SMITH

Scenic Design by
BARRY AXTELL

Lighting Design by
SUSAN A. WHITE

*Musical Direction
and Arrangements by*
MICHAEL RICE

General Management
ROGER ALAN GINDI

Press Representative
**SHIRLEY HERZ
ASSOCIATES**

Production Stage Manager
TREY HUNT

Associate Producer
JAY CARDWELL

Originally presented by The Baldwin Theatre.

A BIT OF BACKGROUND INFORMATION

The Order of the Little Sisters of Hoboken was founded in the seventh century by Saint Wilfred, a bishop of England. He established the first convent and school known as the Wilfrid Academy. His motto was "We don't teach beauty—we radiate it!" Many years later a small group of pioneering sisters set out for America to establish a motherhouse in Cleveland. But they got off the plane in Newark by mistake. The order was "found" by the Newark Airport Police and the new motherhouse was established in Hoboken, New Jersey. It was at that time that the Order of St. Wilfrid elected to change the name to the Little Sisters of Hoboken and they have been affectionately known as the "Little Hobos" ever since. It was from this convent that Sister Mary Cardelia, Sister Mary Hubert and Sister Robert Anne, set sail for the Mediterranean to establish their leper colony. Today the order has both nuns and brothers as members—all doing various good works in the Diocese of Newark. They also operate Mount Saint Helen's School in Hoboken.

TIME: The Present

PLACE: Mt. Saint Helen's School Auditorium

MUSICAL NUMBERS AND SCENES
ACT I

Welcome .... Sr. Mary Cardelia
"Nunsense Is Habit-Forming" .... Cast
Opening remarks .... Srs. Cardelia and Hubert
"A Difficult Transition" .... Cast
The Quiz .... Sr. Mary Amnesia
"Benedicite" .... Sr. Mary Leo
"The Biggest Ain't the Best" .... Sr. Mary Hubert and Sr. Mary Leo
"Playing Second Fiddle" .... Sr. Robert Anne
Taking Responsibility .... Sr. Mary Cardelia
"So You Want to Be a Nun" .... Sr. Mary Amnesia
A Word from the Reverend Mother .... Sr. Mary Cardelia
"Turn Up the Spotlight" .... Sr. Mary Cardelia
"Lilacs Bring Back Memories" ...... Srs. Cardelia, Hubert, Leo & Amnesia
An Unexpected Discovery .... Sr. Mary Cardelia
"Tackle That Temptation with a Time Step" .... Cast

THERE WILL BE ONE TEN-MINUTE INTERMISSION.

ACT II

Robert to the Rescue .... Sr. Robert Anne
"Growing Up Catholic" .... Srs. Robert Anne, Leo, Hubert & Amnesia
"We've Got to Clean out the Freezer" .... Cast
A Minor Catastrophe .... Cast
"Just a Coupl'a Sisters" .... Srs. Cardelia and Hubert
"Soup's On" (The Dying Nun Ballet) .... Sr. Mary Leo
Baking with the BVM .... Sr. Julia, Child of God
"Playing Second Fiddle" (Reprise) .... Sr. Robert Anne
"I Just Want to Be a Star" .... Sr. Robert Anne
"The Drive In" .... Srs. Robert Anne, Amnesia & Leo
A Home Movie .... Cast
"I Could've Gone to Nashville" .... Sr. Mary Amnesia
"Gloria in Excelsis Deo" .... Cast
Closing Remarks .... Sr. Mary Cardelia & Cast
"Holier Than Thou" .... Sr. Mary Hubert & Cast
"Nunsense Is Habit-Forming" (Reprise) .... Cast

MUSICIANS

Conductor, Piano .... Michael Rice
Synthesizer .... Sande Campbell
Woodwinds .... David Henderson
Drums and Percussion .... Grace Millan

UNDERSTUDIES
Understudies never substitute for listed players unless a specific announcement for the appearance is made at the time of the performance.

Understudy—Susan Gordon-Clark

Prior to entering the convent:

SISTER MARY CARDELIA was MARILYN FARINA
SISTER MARY HUBERT was VICKI BELMONTE
SISTER ROBERT ANNE was CHRISTINE ANDERSON
SISTER MARY AMNESIA was SEMINA DE LAURENTIS
SISTER MARY LEO was SUZI WINSON

7

A NOTE FROM THE AUTHOR

I spent a great deal of my life around nuns. And most of my experiences left wonderful memories. I wrote "Nunsense" because I wanted to share what I knew to be "the humor of the nun." Though it may be hard to believe after you read this script, each of the Little Sisters of Hoboken is based on a *real-life* nun.

SISTER MARY REGINA was to the outside world a model Mother Superior even if she was overweight. But to those who knew her, she was an outrageous, quick-witted soul who knew how to get a laugh. She tried to convince you that she was strict, but everyone knew that her "bark was worse than her bite!"

SISTER MARY HUBERT was a kind person who would always try to be understanding and diplomatic. She taught the Novices the ground rules, and was supposed to be dignified. But with the slightest bit of encouragement she was ready to kick up her heels.

SISTER ROBERT ANNE was a tough streetwise nun who had a heart of gold. All the kids adored her because she spoke their language. And she could hit a baseball "out of the park."

SISTER MARY AMNESIA was the picture of innocence. She couldn't remember her past and so looked at each new day with a childlike joy.

SR. MARY LEO had been a professional dancer before she entered the convent and was always eager to display her talent. She was very impressionable because she was young and could easily be led astray.

In the context of *"Nunsense,"* Sister Mary Regina (Reverend Mother), Sister Mary Hubert, and Sister Robert Anne are the only nuns who actually worked in the Leper Colony. Sister Mary Amnesia and Sister Mary Leo only know of the Leper Colony through stories told by the others. Reverend Mother and Sister Hubert have a healthy rivalry (somewhat like Mame Dennis and Vera Charles in "Auntie Mame"). Each is always trying to outdo the other. But, Reverend Mother is always quick to remind everyone that she *is* the Mother Superior. Sister Robert Anne is

Reverend Mother's nemesis. She would probably be thrown out of the convent if it weren't for the fact that Reverend Mother really knows that Sister Robert Anne is, underneath it all, a very dedicated nun. Everyone likes Sister Mary Amnesia because she is so innocent. Except for her first entrance when she appears a bit shy, she is unafraid. When she realizes that the audience is friendly nothing can dampen her childlike enthusiasm. Sister Mary Leo is frustrated by Reverend Mother in her attempt to shine as a nun-ballerina. For this reason she is easily led astray by her "buddy" Sister Robert Anne.

Before the performance and during intermission the sisters wander through the auditorium, on the stage, etc., as they please. For, after all, they are in their own school. They are very much "at home." As the performance progresses they become equally "at home" in the spotlight!

The script indicates that the sisters are performing on the set of the "eighth grade production of *Grease*," and they are accompanied by a band. However, it should be noted, that the sisters could just as easily present their "benefit" in a church basement with an old upright piano and no set at all. "Nunsense" is a musical comedy for everyone — everywhere!

Dan Goggin

CAST OF CHARACTERS

SISTER MARY REGINA, MOTHER SUPERIOR — A feisty overweight Sophie Tucker-type who can't resist the spotlight.

SISTER MARY HUBERT, MISTRESS OF NOVICES — The second in command, she is always competing with the Mother Superior.

SISTER ROBERT ANNE — A streetwise tough character from Brooklyn. A constant source of aggravation for the Mother Superior.

SISTER MARY AMNESIA — This nun lost her memory after a crucifix fell on her head. She is very sweet.

SISTER MARY LEO — The novice, who has entered the convent with the firm desire to become the first nun ballerina.

NOTE:

In the Original New York Production the Mother Superior was named SISTER MARY CARDELIA. In all subsequent productions the Mother Superior is named SISTER MARY REGINA, while SISTER MARY CARDELIA is the nun who modeled for the convent greeting cards.

TIME: The Present

PLACE: Mt. Saint Helen's School Auditorium

MUSICAL NUMBERS AND SCENES

ACT ONE

Welcome . . . . Sr. Mary Regina
"Nunsense Is Habit-Forming" . . . . Cast
Opening remarks . . . . Srs. Regina and Hubert
"A Difficult Transition" . . . . Cast
The Quiz . . . . Sr. Mary Amnesia
"Benedicite" . . . . Sr. Mary Leo
"The Biggest Ain't the Best" . . . . Srs. Hubert and Leo
"Playing Second Fiddle" . . . . Sr. Robert Anne
Taking Responsibility . . . . Sr. Mary Regina
"So You Want to Be a Nun" . . . . Sr. Mary Amnesia
A Word from the Reverend Mother . . . . Sr. Mary Regina
"Turn Up the Spotlight" . . . . Sr. Mary Regina
"Lilacs Bring Back Memories" . . . . . Srs. Regina, Hubert, Leo &
Amnesia
An Unexpected Discovery . . . . Sr. Mary Regina
"Tackle That Temptation with a Time Step" . . . Sr. Mary Hubert
& Cast

ACT TWO

Robert to the Rescue . . . . Sr. Robert Anne
"Growing Up Catholic" . . . . . . Srs. Robert Anne, Leo, Hubert &
Amnesia
"We've Got to Clean out the Freezer" . . . . Cast
A Minor Catastrophe . . . . Cast
"Just a Coupl'a Sisters" . . . . Srs. Regina and Hubert
"Soup's On" (The Dying Nun Ballet) . . . . Sr. Mary Leo
Baking with the BVM . . . . Sr. Julia, Child of God
"Playing Second Fiddle" (Reprise) . . . . Sr. Robert Anne
"I Just Want to Be a Star" . . . . Sr. Robert Anne
"The Drive In" . . . . Srs. Robert Anne, Amnesia & Leo
A Home Movie . . . . Cast
"I Could've Gone to Nashville" . . . . Sr. Mary Amnesia
"Gloria in Excelsis Deo" . . . . Cast
Closing Remarks . . . . Sr. Mary Regina & Cast
"Holier Than Thou" . . . . Sr. Mary Hubert & Cast
"Nunsense Is Habit-Forming" (Reprise) . . . . Cast

11

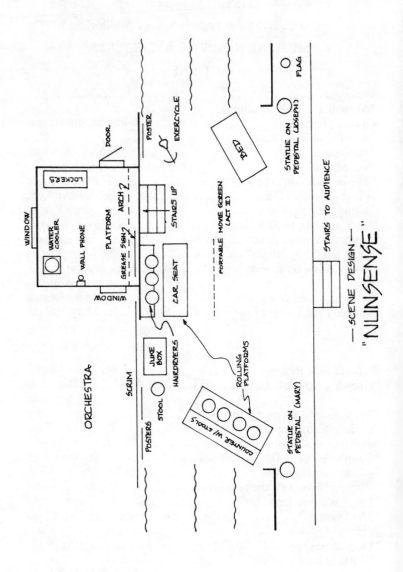

— SCENE DESIGN —
"NUNSENSE"

Nunsense

PROLOGUE

*The stage is set according to the ground plan (opposite). In addi-
tion, the easel announcing the benefit is placed center stage
and a basketball is placed on the stage in a random position
as if left by accident.*

[MUSIC CUE 1: PUBLIC DOMAIN SELECTIONS]

*The MUSICIANS enter. They are attired as part of the religious
community. They begin playing "public domain" selections
which have been chosen by the CONDUCTOR. SISTERS
ROBERT ANNE, MARY LEO, and MARY HUBERT come
into the auditorium and begin visiting with members of the
audience. After a few minutes, REVEREND MOTHER
enters with the STAGE MANAGER who is also in religious
garb. REVEREND MOTHER surveys the situation and
suddenly notices the poster of Marilyn Monroe in the bathing suit. She is visibly upset and orders the STAGE MAN-
AGER to get the black "drape" hanging on the easel which
she affixes to the poster making a skirt to cover Marilyn. All
of this is done in an ad libbed fashion without concern for
the audience. REVEREND MOTHER is simply preparing
for the show which is about to begin. The STAGE MAN-
AGER or one of the nuns removes the easel as another picks
up the basketball and gets it offstage. (If basketball hoops
are being used as part of the set, someone may shoot a
basket.)*

*The STAGE MANAGER then takes his/her post to call the
show and REVEREND MOTHER starts clicking her "frog
clicker" to summon the other sisters to the stage. SISTER
MARY HUBERT sits at the lunch counter; SISTER ROB-
ERT ANNE takes a seat under one of the hair dryers; and
SISTER MARY LEO sits on the exercycle. REVEREND
MOTHER orders the musicians to stop playing and we hear
SISTER HUBERT say:*

13

SR. HUBERT. Get Amnesia. Reverend Mother, where's Amnesia?

REV. MOTHER. Sister . . . Sister Amnesia. (*REV. MOTHER goes up the steps to the door.*) Come on out, Sister. It's okay.

(*SR. AMNESIA enters* U. *as REV. MOTHER brings her down the steps and seats her next to SR. ROBERT ANNE. REV. MOTHER then moves center stage and signals the spotlight operator to put the spot on her. The light comes on at knee level. REV. MOTHER, very irritatedly, motions to get the light on her face. As the light comes on her face she smiles and Act One begins.*)

ACT ONE

REV. MOTHER. Good evening, friends. On behalf of the Little Sisters of Hoboken, I'd like to say: "Welcome to the theatre — of Mount Saint Helen's School!" And may I extend our gratitude to each and everyone of you for coming here this evening to participate in our fund-raising activities. Now, before we begin, I want to clear up what seems to be some confusion about the set here. You see, our eighth graders are putting on the musical "Vaseline" and I gave —

SR. HUBERT. (*Interrupting, she whispers and points to the sign hanging behind REV. MOTHER.*) It's *Grease.*

REV. MOTHER. Oh — it's "Grease!" Well, anyway, I promised the children that we wouldn't disturb their handiwork during our benefit and so that's why things may seem a little incongruous at times.

Now, we have a wonderful introductory song, but before we begin the festivities, let us ask the Lord to bless our endeavors. Sister, if you will.

[MUSIC CUE 2: "VENI CREATOR SPIRITUS"]

SR. ROBERT ANNE.
VENI CREATOR SPIRITUS.
ALL.
MENTES TUORUM VISITA.
IMPLE SUPERNA GRATIA,
QUAE TU CREASTI PECTORA.

[MUSIC CUE 3: "NUNSENSE IS HABIT-FORMING"]

ALL.
SOME FOLKS THINK OF CONVENTS
AS THE PLACES WHERE WE PRAY.
BUT LET US TELL YOU CONVENTS
ARE MUCH MORE THAN THAT TODAY.

WE'RE DEDICATED PEOPLE
BUT WE LIKE TO HAVE OUR FUN.
REV. MOTHER.
WE'RE HERE TONIGHT TO SHARE WITH YOU
THE HUMOR OF THE NUN!

ALL.
NUNSENSE IS HABIT-FORMING,
LET US TELL YOU WHY.
REV. MOTHER.
WHEN A SISTER GETS APPLAUSE,
IT'S A SPECIAL "HIGH."
ALL.
THERE IS NOTHING WE CAN DO
ONCE WE GET A LAUGH OR TWO.
IT'S SOMETHING WE CANNOT CONTROL
ONCE WE'RE ON A ROLL!
SR. ROBERT ANNE.
HAVE YOU HEARD THE ONE ABOUT THE TRAVELING
   SALESNUN
WHO REALLY DREW A CROWD?
IT SEEMS THIS FARMER HAD A HORSE
RATHER WELL-ENDOWED—
REV. MOTHER.
SISTER! NUNSENSE MAY BE HABIT-FORMING
BUT LET'S DRAW THE LINE!
SR. HUBERT.
CUT THE CHEAP SHOTS!
WHY BE COMMON?
REV. MOTHER.
WE CAN BE DIVINE!
ALL.
EVERYBODY'S HERE SO LET'S TELL THEM WHO WE
   ARE:
REV. MOTHER.
THIS IS SISTER ROBERT ANNE.
SHE SINGS AND DRIVES THE CAR.
SISTER MARY AMNESIA
DOESN'T KNOW HER REAL NAME.
ALL but SR. AMNESIA.
A CRUCIFIX FELL ON HER HEAD.
HER MEMORY'S GONE, WHAT A SHAME!
SR. ROBERT ANNE.
SISTER HUBERT IS OUR NOVICE MISTRESS
AND OUR GUIDING LIGHT.
SR. LEO.
SHE'S SECOND IN COMMAND
AND STANDS AT REVEREND MOTHER'S RIGHT.

Sr. Hubert.
SISTER LEO IS THE YOUNGEST.
AS A NOVICE, SHE'S BRAND NEW.
  Rev. Mother.
AND I'M YOUR REVEREND MOTHER
SISTER MARY REGINA, THAT'S WHO!
  All.
NUNSENSE IS HABIT-FORMING,
THAT'S WHAT PEOPLE SAY.
WE'RE HERE TO PROVE THAT NUNS ARE FUN,
PERHAPS A BIT RISQUE.

WE STILL WEAR OUR HABITS
TO RETAIN OUR MAGIC SPELL.
AND THOUGH WE'RE ON OUR WAY TO HEAVEN,
WE'RE HERE TO RAISE SOME HELL!
  Rev. Mother. Sell it, girls!
  All.
NUNSENSE IS HABIT-FORMING,
THAT'S THE REASON WE
ARE UP HERE ON THE STAGE TONIGHT
HOPING YOU'LL AGREE.
  Rev. Mother, Sr. Robert Anne, Sr. Hubert.
NUNSENSE IS HABIT-FORMING.
  Sr. Leo, Sr. Amnesia.
WE'RE HOOKED!
  All.
AND ALL WE KNOW IS:
WE JUST CAN'T KICK IT,
THOUGH SOME FOLKS MAY PICKET,
WE JUST CAN'T KICK THIS NUNSENSE
SO ON WITH THE SHOW!

(*Quick blackout. Lights up. All of the sisters are congratulating
    each other as SR. ROBERT ANNE, SR. AMNESIA, and
    SR. LEO exit* R. *SR. HUBERT is* C. *on "Reverend Mother's
    right."*)

Rev. Mother. Oh, thank-you. Thank-you so very much.
Now, just in case there is anyone here who hasn't heard what our
little fund-raiser is all about — we've had a small disaster back at
our convent. You see, a short time ago, our cook, Sister Julia —

Child of God (*BOTH cross themselves.*) served some vichyssoise soup and nearly every sister died instantly of botulism!

SR. HUBERT. It was kind of like the "Last Supper!" (*pause*) That's a little convent humor.

REV. MOTHER. Why, we wouldn't be alive tonight if it hadn't been for the fact that we were off playing bingo with some Maryknolls. (*to SR. HUBERT*) What a bunch of cut-throats they turned out to be, huh?

SR. HUBERT. (*very excitedly*) I still say their Mother Superior cheated when she didn't call B-15! I know she had it and then—

REV. MOTHER. (*interrupting*) Calm down, Sister. (*to audience*) The point is when we got back to the convent we found fifty-two of our sisters lying face down in that soup!

SR. HUBERT. Now, we had no idea what to do so we all began praying for guidance.

REV. MOTHER. Then I had a vision! It was either Saint Catherine of Siena or Saint Thomas Aquinas in drag! Anyway, I was instructed to use our own Sister Mary Cardelia as a model and start a greeting card company to raise funds. Well, of course, I did—and it was a huge success!

SR. HUBERT. So we took the money and buried 48 of the 52 dead sisters and then Reverend Mother bought a Beta-Max for the convent! (*pause*) Personally, I thought we should have buried all of the sisters before we bought the Beta-Max, but then as Mistress of Novices, I'm only "number two" so one tries hard not to question Reverend Mother.

REV. MOTHER and SR. HUBERT. (*REV. MOTHER is glaring at SR. HUBERT.*) And one will try harder in the future.

REV. MOTHER. That's right, dear. (*REV. MOTHER, using both hands with index fingers extended, makes a pointing motion to the floor as if to punctuate her sentence.*) The important fact is that we had to put the last four sisters in the freezer.

SR. HUBERT. And, Sister Julia—Child of God (*They cross themselves.*) is having a fit about that.

REV. MOTHER. So that's why we're putting on this little show. We've got to raise enough money to bury those last four dead sisters!

SR. HUBERT. We hope you'll forgive the limitations put on us by the loss of so many of our sisters, but if they hadn't *died*, we wouldn't have to *bury* them, and then there wouldn't *be* this little show in the first place.

REV. MOTHER. (*rather irritatedly*) But, *they* did, *we* have to, and there *is*, so *there* you are! (*They turn to each other and do the "pointed finger punctuation gesture" simultaneously. REV. MOTHER immediately goes back to addressing the audience.*) Now, about a week ago I held tryouts for tonight's show and I chose the sisters whom I felt were the very best of what's left of us. And I asked each of them to prepare something that best displayed her talent.

SR. HERBERT. But first, I thought you might be interested in knowing some of the history of the Little Sisters of Hoboken and that is what our next song is all about. (*SR. HUBERT goes to summon the others who enter* R. *as REV. MOTHER continues talking to the audience.*)

REV. MOTHER. You see, we started out running a leper colony. Oh, now I know you probably think that's a bit distasteful, but all of the *good* causes were taken! You see, it all began when we—(*REV. MOTHER sees that the other sisters are ready to sing.*) Well, if I give it all away you won't enjoy the song. What do you say we just do it! (*REV. MOTHER nods to the CONDUCTOR.*)

CONDUCTOR. Five, six, seven, eight!

[MUSIC CUE 4: "A DIFFICULT TRANSITION"]

ALL.
AVE MARIA! IT'S SO HEAVENLY TO BE A
MEMBER OF A GROUP THAT'S PUTTIN' ON A SHOW!
SR. ROBERT ANNE.
IT'S GREAT!
ALL.
ALTHOUGH IT IS A DIFFICULT TRANSITION
FOR WE STARTED OFF AS MISSIONARIES
WHICH, OF COURSE, IS OBVIOUSLY
MUCH MORE APPROPOS.
SR. AMNESIA.
BUT THEIR MISSION GOT IN TROUBLE.
SR. LEO.
AND THAT BURST THEIR HOLY BUBBLE.
REV. MOTHER.
WE WERE CAUGHT IN AN IMBROGLIO,
SR. HUBERT.
AND WE FINALLY HAD TO GO.

ALL.
SO WE HOPE YOU'LL UNDERSTAND
IF WE'RE NOT ABSOLUTELY GRAND.
SR. AMNESIA and SR. LEO.
FOR WE FEEL A LITTLE QUEASY,
ALL.
WE'RE UNEASY IN THIS SHOW.
REV. MOTHER. Let me start from the beginning. Now pay attention! We're going to give you the history of our order and you're going to be quizzed on it afterward!
FILLED WITH GREAT ANXIETY
SISTER HUBERT SAILED WITH ME
AND SISTER ROBERT ANNE
TO A LAND OF UNKNOWN CIRCUMSTANCE.

WE REACHED OUR DESTINATION
WITH A BIT OF TREPIDATION
FOR WE'D COME TO ORDER LEPERS
BACK TO WORK IN SOUTHERN FRANCE.
SR. ROBERT ANNE.
NO!
SR. HUBERT.
NO!
SR. LEO.
NO!
SR. AMNESIA.
NO!
REV. MOTHER. Oh, no! That's not right! We'd come to join an order *working* with lepers on an island *south* of France! That's it!
ALL.
EACH OF US, AS BEST WE COULD,
CUT A TREE AND CHOPPED SOME WOOD
WHICH THEN WAS USED IN BUILDING
HUMBLE HUTS FOR QUARANTINE.

WHEN SISTER MARK YVONNE
HAD FINISHED UP THE PORTA-JOHN,
WE ALL SAT DOWN AND WAITED
FOR THE FIRST OF THOSE UNCLEAN.
REV. MOTHER. And they came from everywhere!

Sr. Robert Anne.
THERE WERE HOTTENTOTS WITH ROTTEN TOTS
IN BASKETS ON EACH MOTHER'S HEAD.
Sr. Amnesia and Sr. Leo.
AND ZULUS, THEY CONCLUDED
NEVER UNDERSTOOD A THING THEY SAID.
Sr. Hubert.
UBANGIS WHO WERE GANGING UP
ON NATIVES WHO WERE BEING FED,
Sr. Robert Anne.
AND SWAZI WHO WERE GOOSING
ALL THE BUSHMEN IN THE LINE AHEAD.
All.
IT WAS DREADFUL!

THE PYGMIES HAD THEIR NOSES
STUCK IN EVERYBODY'S BUSINESS
WHILE WATUSIS HAD THEIR BUSINESS
STUCK IN EVERYBODY'S NOSE.
BUT THE TRUTH OF THE MATTER,
IF YOU REALLY WANT TO KNOW,
WAS THAT EVERYBODY'S BUSINESS
WAS ABOUT TO DECOMPOSE.
Rev. Mother.
HUBERT, ROBERT ANNE, AND I
ARE LUCKY THAT WE'RE STILL ALIVE
FOR SISTERS WENT TO PIECES
AT A DEVASTATING RATE.

WHEN A NOVICE SPILLED HER FOOD,
AT FIRST, WE THOUGHT HER RATHER CRUDE
TILL WE REALIZED HER HAND
WAS ON THE FLOOR WITH HER FORK AND HER
PLATE!
All. Wait!
Rev. Mother. There's more!
Sr. Hubert.
THE PROTESTANTS, IT SEEMS,
HAD SET OUT TO WRECK OUR DREAMS.
All.
WE HAD HUMBLE HUTS
WHILE THEY BUILT LEPER CONDOS-BY-THE-SEA.

Rev. Mother.
COMPETING FOR EACH LEPER
PUT OUR MISSION WORK IN JEOPARDY.
SO WE DEVISED A PLAN
TO AVOID CATASTROPHE.

Sr. Hubert.
WE CHALLENGED THEM TO RACE
CAUSE WE THOUGHT WE'D TRUMP THEIR ACE
IN THE HUNDRED METER DASH
WHEN WE ENTERED SISTER ROSE.

Sr. Robert Anne.
BUT AS SHE WAS VICTORY-BOUND,
HER SCHNOZ FELL ON THE GROUND.

All.
IF IT HADN'T FALLEN OFF,
SHE'D HAVE WON IT BY A NOSE!

Rev. Mother.
POOR ROSE!

All.
OOOOHHHH!

Rev. Mother.
HUBERT, ROBERT ANNE, AND I
HAD MANAGED ONCE MORE TO SURVIVE.
BUT THIS TIME WE KNEW
WE WERE IN A TRULY HOPELESS SPOT.

Sr. Robert Anne.
SO WE PACKED UP WHAT WAS LEFT,
FEELING TOTALLY BEREFT,
AND GOT OUT WHILE THE GOING
WAS STILL ABLE TO BE GOT.

Rev. Mother, Sr. Robert Anne, and Sr. Hubert.
WE CAME BACK HOME TO HOBOKEN
BUT WITH SPIRITS SO BROKEN
NO ONE REALLY KNEW
IF WE'D PULL THROUGH.

Sr. Amnesia and Sr. Leo.
THEN REVEREND MOTHER PRAYED
THERE WOULD BE A NEW CRUSADE.

All.
AND WE WERE DOING GREAT
TILL SISTER JULIA MADE THAT STEW!
(*Eyes heavenward.*) MON DIEU!
AVE MARIA! IT'S SO HEAVENLY TO BE A

Rev. Mother.
MOTHER!
   Sr. Robert Anne, Sr. Hubert, and Sr. Leo.
SISTER!
   Sr. Amnesia.
SISTER! (*REV. MOTHER gives SR. AMNESIA the eye for not singing "sister" with the others.*)
   All.
MAKING A DEBUT IN FRONT OF YOU.
IT'S A DIFFICULT TRANSITION
FOR THE MISSIONER'S POSITION
WAS UP TILL NOW THE ONLY ONE WE KNEW,
IT'S SAD, BUT TRUE.

SO WE HOPE YOU'LL UNDERSTAND
IF WE'RE NOT ABSOLUTELY GRAND.
BUT WE WILL DO OUR BEST
TO SEE THAT YOU'RE IMPRESSED.
WE HOPE WE'LL PASS THE TEST.
NOW THE REST IS UP TO YOU! AMEN!

(*Quick blackout. Lights up.*)

(*REV. MOTHER and SR. HUBERT seem to be taking center stage as SR. LEO exits L. and SR. ROBERT ANNE and SR. AMNESIA are exiting R.*)

   Sr. Hubert. (*as she sees SR. AMNESIA leaving*) Sister Amnesia. Sister Amnesia, where are you going?
   Sr. Amnesia. I was just going with her. (*She points to the exit where SR. ROBERT ANNE went.*)
   Sr. Hubert. But, aren't you in charge of the quiz?
   Sr. Amnesia. Oh, I forgot! (*She runs up the stairs to the lockers where she gets a ruler.*)
   Sr. Hubert. I just can't seem to get through to her, Reverend Mother.
   Rev. Mother. I know. I keep hoping if she remembers who she is, we'll discover she belongs to the Franciscans. (*REV. MOTHER exits L. as SR. AMNESIA returns from the lockers.*)
   Sr. Hubert. Now, Sister Amnesia, try to remember what I teach in the novitiate: Gentle, but *firm*! (*SR. HUBERT exits L.*)
   Sr. Amnesia. (*repeating*) Gentle, but *firm*! (*She snaps to at-*

tention, holding her ruler in hand. She paces for a moment or two and then comes D.C.)

Alright! Sit up straight! Eyes forward! Pay attention! Do you know what time it is? (*She hits the palm of her hand with her ruler. It obviously hurts and she grimaces. She immediately reverts to her wide-eyed innocent self.*) You know, I *always* know what time it is. Cause you see, back at the convent we have this huge clock with the Twelve Apostles pasted on it. And I always know when the big hand is on the John and the little hand is on the Peter it is time for the Sisters to go down on their knees. (*pause*) And pray!

And now it's time for that quiz that Reverend Mother warned you about. (*She takes the index cards out of her pocket and hooks the ruler onto her belt.*) Okay! Here are the questions that you should have the answers to if you were paying attention to that last song. Could I have some lights, please? (*House lights up.*) Thank-you!

Now, if you know the answer you raise your hand. Are you ready? (*She waits for a response. If none, she asks again.*) Are you ready? Good!

Question number one: The leper colony was established on an island south of _____.

(*She either calls on someone who has a raised hand, or if everyone responds "France!" she will reprimand the group for not raising hands and then select a person who gave the right answer.*)

[MUSIC CUE 5: QUIZ FANFARE]

(*The Fanfare is played whenever the right answer is heard by the CONDUCTOR, whether by the group or an individual.)*

(*SR. AMNESIA goes into the audience to the winner.*) I have a prize for you. (*She takes a prize out of the pocket in her tunic. The first prize given out must be something involving St. Christopher.*) It's a Saint Christopher (key ring, medal, holy card, etc.)! Now, I know St. Christopher is no longer a saint, but we got a whole bunch of them at a huge discount. (*She gives the prize to the winner and returns to center stage.*)

Okay, question number two. This is harder than the first one. Why—why did the Sisters leave the leper colony?

[MUSIC CUE 5A: QUIZ TIMER]

(*The timer music plays until SR. AMNESIA hears the correct answer.*)

(*The answer is "they lost the race to the Protestants." But Sister usually accepts anything to do with the Protestants building the condos in the interest of keeping the show's pace up.*)

[MUSIC CUE 5B: QUIZ FANFARE]

(*As before, the Fanfare is played when the correct answer is heard, or when SR. AMNESIA indicates an answer is "close enough!"*)

(*Again she goes into the audience and gives a prize. As she is returning to the stage she will say something like: "How many Catholics do we have here tonight?"* (*She waits for a show of hands, and then selects someone who will receive a prize.*) "I'm going to give you a prize just for being Catholic!" (*She returns to the stage.*)

Now I have one last question that Sister Hubert wanted me to ask: Do you think it was wrong for Reverend Mother to buy a Beta-Max before all of the Sisters were buried? (*REV. MOTHER comes rushing on L. and whisks SR. AMNESIA off R.*)

[MUSIC CUE 5C: QUIZ FANFARE]

REV. MOTHER. (*REV. MOTHER returns to C.*) Well, I think that's about enough time on the quiz! Now, I'd like to present Sister Mary Leo with her interpretation of "Morning at the Convent." Sister—

[MUSIC CUE 6: "BENEDICITE"]

(*REV. MOTHER exits R. SR. LEO enters L. wearing a bathrobe and huge fluffy slippers which are covering her pointe shoes. She sits on the edge of the bed and sings.*)

"BENEDICITE"

SR. LEO.
I WAKE UP ALL BLEARY

WHEN I FIRST HEAR THE
AGE OLD QUERY:

SR. HUBERT. (*enters* L. *slightly in view of audience*)
Benedicite. (*pronounced* Ben-ay-DEE-chee-tay) (*SR. HUBERT
exits* L. *immediately.*)

SR. LEO. Dominus. (*pronounced* DOH-mee-noos)
THANK GOD WE CAN'T SPEAK TO EACH OTHER,
I'M NOT IN THE MOOD TO BE CHEERY!
(*She stands and removes the robe. She is underdressed in her
habit.*)
PUT ON THE TUNIC AND SCAPULAR.
THEN THE WIMPLE—LOOK! NO MIRROR!
THE GUIMPE (*pronounced* gamp) AND VEIL
COMPLETE THE NUN'S COUTURE.

(*She sits back down on the bed.*)
AT AN UNGODLY HOUR
THE BELL IN THE TOWER
SIGNALS A WARNING
(*The bell on the wall rings.*)
WE'VE MADE IT THROUGH
ONE MORE NIGHT.
IT'S TIME TO GREET A NEW MORNING.
BUT BEFORE I GO DOWNSTAIRS
I CLEAR MY HEAD OF WOES AND CARES
BY DANCING MY WAY
THROUGH MY MORNING PRAYERS.

(*She removes the slippers and does a dance on pointe.*)

DANCING IS THE WAY I PRAY.
I CAN HAVE A PERFECT DAY,
IF I START OFF WITH A TOUR JETE!
SO IF YOU WAKE UP FEELING BLAH,
TRY MY PROVEN FORMULA.
POINTE YOUR TOES AND PLIÉ,
ONCE EACH DAY!

[MUSIC CUE 6A: BENEDICITE PLAYOFF]

(*She exits* R. *and returns immediately acknowledging applause.
SR. HUBERT enters* L. *carrying SR. LEO's shoes. Music
out.*)

Sr. Hubert. Sister Mary Leo that was just wonderful. I wish I could dance like you do! (*Taking the shoes from SR. HUBERT, SR. LEO goes and sits on the bed and begins changing her shoes, all the while continuing the conversation.*)

Sr. Leo. Well, you could have seen a lot more but Reverend Mother won't let me wear a tutu.

Sr. Hubert. (*standing near the bed*) Now, you know how Reverend Mother feels about the traditional habit.

Sr. Leo. I know. "If God had wanted everyone to look like people,

Sr. Leo and Sr. Hubert. He wouldn't have invented nuns!" (*They both do the "punctuation gesture" with index fingers mocking REV. MOTHER.*)

Sr. Hubert. That's right.

Sr. Leo. But when I entered the convent I planned to dedicate my life to God through the dance. If I can't wear a tutu, I'll never become a famous ballerina!

[MUSIC CUE 7: "THE BIGGEST AIN'T THE BEST"]

Sr. Hubert. Sister Leo! Have we forgotten about humility? (*SR. LEO looks embarrassed. SR. HUBERT moves D.C. and sings directly to the audience.*)

"THE BIGGEST AIN'T THE BEST"

I'VE ALWAYS TAUGHT THE NOVICES
THAT GOD IS ON THEIR SIDE,
WHEN THEY'RE LOOKING FOR THE STRENGTH
TO AVOID THE SIN OF PRIDE.

Sr. Leo. (*Sitting on the bed, SR. LEO responds.*)
I KNOW THAT BEING HUMBLE
IS A VIRTUE WE HOLD DEAR.
BUT HOW CAN I BE HUMBLE
AND ADVANCE IN MY CAREER?

Sr. Hubert. Sister Mary Leo! Your vocation *is* your career! (*to audience*) Would you excuse me for a moment? (*She goes and sits on the bed next to SR. LEO.*) Sister, I'd like to say something before this goes any further. You see, I wanted to be a nun ever since I was a little girl. My dream was to enter the convent, work my way up to Mother Superior, and then turn the Little Sisters of Hoboken into (*She stands and with great gusto says:*) the Big Sisters of Newark! Well, the first lesson I had to learn upon entering the convent was that we do not strive for position — just perfection. Besides, she who exaults herself shall be humbled and she who humbles herself shall be exalted! (*She sits back down on the bed.*)

REVEREND MOTHER IS THE BOSS
AND SO I MUST OBEY.
BUT AS THE MISTRESS OF THE NOVICES
I SHINE IN MY OWN WAY.
   Sr. Leo.
YOU MEAN, IF I'M REALLY HUMBLE
I COULD HAVE A SHOT
AT A BIT OF EXALTATION
WITH MY SIMPLE LOT?
   Sr. Hubuert.
You got it, kid!

THE BIGGEST AIN'T THE BEST.
VERY OFTEN WE'RE IMPRESSED
BY A TINY DIAMOND CHIP
THAT SEEMS TO OUTSHINE ALL THE REST.

SO PAY ATTENTION NOW.
HERE'S WHAT YOU MUST DO:
DON'T DEMAND THE SPOTLIGHT,
LET THE SPOTLIGHT COME TO YOU.

(*The spotlight comes up on both of them.*)

   Sr. Leo. I'm beginning to see the light.
   Sr. Hubert.
REMEMBER SISTER HILDA
WHOSE ENDOWMENT WAS SO GREAT?
   Sr. Leo.
WHEN SHE PUT ON HER COLLAR
IT STOOD OUT LIKE A PLATE.
(*Sr. LEO holds her collar straight out.*)
   Sr. Hubert.
WELL, ONE DAY WHEN THE BISHOP CAME AND
SHE WENT TO THE DOOR,
AS SHE KNELT TO KISS HIS RING
SHE FELL FLAT OUT ON THE FLOOR

(*SR. HUBERT falls forward off the bed.*)
AND PROVED:
  Sr. Hubert and Sr. Leo.
THE BIGGEST AIN'T THE BEST
AS THE BISHOP WILL ATTEST.
(*SR. LEO helps SR. HUBERT off the floor.*)
THE LORD TELLS US THE LEAST
ARE OFTEN THOSE THAT ARE THE BLEST.
  Sr. Hubert.
SO LET THAT BE A LESSON TO YOU,
TRY TO UNDERSTAND.
THE PEOPLE WITH THE BIGGEST DRUMS
DON'T ALWAYS LEAD THE BAND!
  Sr. Hubert and Sr. Leo.
(*SR. HUBERT motions to SR. LEO and they move D.C.*)
OH, THE BIGGEST AIN'T THE BEST.
VERY OFTEN WE'RE IMPRESSED
BY A TINY DIAMOND CHIP
THAT SEEMS TO OUTSHINE ALL THE REST.
  Sr. Hubert.
SO DO WHAT YOU DO WELL.
  Sr. Leo.
I KNOW I'LL BE FINE. (*She crosses herself.*)
  Sr. Hubert.
JUST REMEMBER TO BE HUMBLE.
(*SR. LEO kneels on the floor for a second.*)
  Sr. Hubert and Sr. Leo.
AS WE PROUDLY GO AND—
  Sr. Hubert.
Smile, baby!
  Sr. Leo.
Sparkle, Neely!
  Sr. Hubert and Sr. Leo.
Sing out, Louise!
AND SHINE!

(*REV. MOTHER enters R. applauding.*)

Rev. Mother. Well, that was just dandy. It sounded just
wonderful backstage.

[MUSIC CUE 8: ROBERT ANNE'S SURPRISE]

(*SR. LEO and SR. HUBERT are trying to say "thank-you" to REV. MOTHER for the compliment as SR. ROBERT ANNE enters* R. *dancing. She has her veil twisted up around her head like a turban with some fruit dangling from it. She is shaking a pair of maracas.*)

SR. ROBERT ANNE. Well, what d'ya think? I call it the "Convent Miranda" look!

(*SR. HUBERT and SR. LEO realize there is going to be trouble and exit* L. *quietly.*)

REV. MOTHER. Sister! I am appalled! Now, you show some respect!

SR. ROBERT ANNE. Oh, cool your jets, Rev. (*She takes down her veil and puts the fruit and maracas on the counter.*) Listen, I've got another little surprise for you.

REV. MOTHER. Another surprise?

SR. ROBERT ANNE. Yeah. I realized that when you arranged the program for tonight you hadn't included a solo for me and so I've been working on a special song and I thought you could find a spot for it in the show. Listen to this. (*SR. ROBERT ANNE nods to the conductor.*)

[MUSIC CUE 8A: ANOTHER SURPRISE]

WHEN I BECAME A NUN AT A VERY EARLY AGE—

REV. MOTHER. (*interrupting*) Sister—Sister! (*Music out.*) Sister Robert Anne, you are the understudy. Do you realize what a great honor and responsibility that is? You must be ready at a moment's notice in case an emergency should arise. Take me, for example. I am the Mother Superior, not a musical comedy star!

[MUSIC CUE 9: "PLAYING SECOND FIDDLE"]

SR. ROBERT ANNE. I realized that from the opening number. (*SR. ROBERT ANNE is amused by her remark while REV. MOTHER is fuming.*) Hey, listen: (*She sings to REV. MOTHER.*)

"PLAYING SECOND FIDDLE"

I DON'T MEAN TO SOUND UNGRATEFUL,

BUT I'D RATHER HAVE A SPOT
THAT IS JUST FOR ROBERT ANNE.
I'M NOT ASKING FOR A LOT.

AN UNDERSTUDY NEVER SHINES
UNTIL THE STAR IS ILL.
THEN THE CROWD IS HOSTILE.
THE STAR'S NOT ON THE BILL!

REV. MOTHER. Sister, I don't believe this is something to discuss in front of the audience.

SR. ROBERT ANNE.
PLAYING SECOND FIDDLE
POSITIVELY MEANS THIS KID'LL
NEVER GET A MOMENT
ON THE STAGE ALONE.
EVEN, GOD FORBID,
IF SOMETHING HAPPENED
AND YOU DID GET SICK—

(*A look of glee comes over SR. ROBERT ANNE's face.*)

REV. MOTHER. Yes?

SR. ROBERT ANNE.
AN UNDERSTUDIED PART
IS NOT MY OWN!

I've been reading up on being an understudy and believe me it's not encouraging! (*She pulls out a booklet titled, "The Understudy," which she has had tucked in her belt under her scapular. She opens it and hands it to REV. MOTHER.*) Here, read!

WHO HERE KNOWS THAT DOLLY LEVI'S
ALSO BIBI OSTERWALD?
CAROL CHANNING WASN'T SICK
SO BIBI WASN'T CALLED.
THIS GIRL, LENORA NEMETZ,
HAS IT ON HER RESUME
THAT SHE UNDERSTUDIED EVERYONE.
WHERE IS SHE TODAY?

REV. MOTHER. (*pointing to a page in the book*) Well, there's Shirley MacLaine!

SR. ROBERT ANNE.
No, no!
SHIRLEY DOESN'T COUNT.

THAT WAS JUST BIZARRE.
CAROL HANEY BREAKS HER LEG
AND SHIRLEY IS A STAR.
BUT THAT'S ABOUT AS RARE
AS LANA TURNER DOWN AT SCHWAB'S.
IT'S A MIRACLE WHEN UNDERSTUDIES
GET THE STARRING JOBS!

    REV. MOTHER. Well, then I'd start prayin' if I were you!
    SR. ROBERT ANNE. For what?
    REV. MOTHER. A miracle!
    SR. ROBERT ANNE.

Oh, give me a break!
PLAYING SECOND FIDDLE
POSITIVELY MEANS THIS KID'LL
NEVER GET A LEAD CAUSE
EVERYBODY KNOWS
WHOEVER UNDERSTUDIED MERMAN
AS THE GYPSY MAMA PERMANENTLY
ENDED UP AS "SECOND HAND ROSE!"

(*Music out.*)

    SR. AMNESIA. (*yelling from offstage*) Reverend Mother, I'm ready!

    REV. MOTHER. I've got to get Amnesia out here for her number. We'll talk about this later.

    SR. ROBERT ANNE. Amnesia?! But my number's ready to go. Just give me—

    REV. MOTHER. (*REV. MOTHER has picked up the fruit and with a shake of the maracas shouts:*) NO!! (*REV. MOTHER exits* R.)

[MUSIC CUE 9A: SECOND FIDDLE CONCLUSION]

    SR. ROBERT ANNE. (*moving* D.C.)
I'VE GOT TO FIGURE OUT A WAY
TO GET A SOLO SPOT,
SO I CAN PROVE TO REVEREND MOTHER
"WHAT IT TAKES," I GOT!
MAYBE THEN SHE'LL UNDERSTAND
THIS FEELING IN MY SOUL
THAT I DESERVE A LEADING ROLE!

(*SR. ROBERT ANNE heads for a seat at the counter as every-one enters* R. *SR. HUBERT sits at the counter and SR. LEO sits on the stool next to the juke box. REV. MOTHER comes* D.C. *with SR. AMNESIA standing behind her.*)

REV. MOTHER. You know, in some ways I feel personally responsible for the predicament that has brought us here tonight. You see, Sister Julia never has been able to get a handle on her vocation. Only last week we had the Monsignor coming over for dinner so I asked Julia to prepare something a little special. A few minutes later I see her in the kitchen settin' up the ironing board. I says, "Julia, what the hell are you doing?" She says, "I'm gonna make pressed duck!" (*A duck call is heard offstage.*)
Come on, folks, it's not easy! We used to have 71 members in our order. But thanks to Julia, we're down to 19! So I thought possibly if you knew a little more about us —
SR. AMNESIA. (*Coming up and tugging on REV. MOTHER's sleeve, she whispers:*) Reverend Mother, I thought I was supposed to do this part.
REV. MOTHER. Oh, my goodness. I'm sorry. I promised Sister here that she could do this part. I'm sorry. Go right ahead, Sister — go on —

[MUSIC CUE 10: "SO YOU WANT TO BE A NUN"]

(*REV. MOTHER goes and sits with the others at the counter. SR. AMNESIA moves* D.C.)

SR. AMNESIA. Hello. My name is Sister Mary — oh, for a moment there I thought I remembered my real name. Anyway, I'm here to tell you what being a nun means to me. (*yelling*) Can you hear me in the back?! Good. Reverend Mother tells me that she is certain that if I give a good talk at least one of you will want to join our order. Well, I think it is just wonderful —

"SO YOU WANT TO BE A NUN?"

THAT YOU WANT TO BE A NUN.
AND YOU THINK IT MIGHT BE FUN
TO BE ONE OF THE ONES WHO'S A NUN.

(*She looks to the others for approval. They nod and she continues.*)

THEN THE ORDER YOU ELECT TO SELECT
SHOULD REFLECT, I SUSPECT
A DESIRE TO PERFECT ALL YOU'VE DONE UP TILL
     NOW.
I WISH THAT SOMEHOW —

(*SISTER MARY ANNETTE suddenly appears sitting atop the hand of SR. AMNESIA. She is a puppet and has been hidden behind SR. AMNESIA's back. SR. AMNESIA using a "different" voice speaks for SISTER MARY ANNETTE. Ventriloquism is optional.*)

SR. M. ANNETTE. Stop!!! I can't stand listening to this!

SR. AMNESIA. Why, Sister Mary Annette! What are you doing here? I thought you stayed in France with the protestants.

SR. M. ANNETTE. No way, Jose. (*to audience*) Girls, if you want to be a nun, join an order that still wears a habit!

SR. AMNESIA. Oh, now wait a minute, Sister. It's true that *we* still wear habits, but even I know that "a habit does not a nun make."

SR. M. ANNETTE. Oh, get real will ya! (*to CONDUCTOR*) Hit it, Schweetheart!

IT'S REALLY VERY SIMPLE WITH A WIMPLE, YOU'LL
     LEARN
YOU GET INSTANT RESPECT WHICH YOU DON'T HAVE
     TO EARN.
YOU MOVE RIGHT UP IN LINES WITHOUT WAITING
     YOUR TURN.
VIRTUES LIKE PATIENCE ARE NOT OUR CONCERN!

SR. AMNESIA. Uh, Sister, I thought virtue was always our concern. (*SR. M. ANNETTE looks at SR. AMNESIA in disbelief.*)

THINK ABOUT THE SOLEMN VOWS.
THERE ARE THREE WE MUST ESPOUSE.
POVERTY, CHASTITY, AND OBEDIENCE,
(*very loudly*) NOW —

SR. M. ANNETTE. What the hell are you trying to do, make me go deaf?

SR. AMNESIA. Don't be silly, Sister. You can't go deaf! Everyone can see nuns don't have ears! Now where was I?

LET'S START WITH POVERTY, EMPTY YOUR PURSE.
POVERTY MAKES BEING POOR EVEN WORSE.
GRANTED, IT'S NOT SO EXTREME FOR A NUN.
WE MAY NOT BE STARVING, BUT STILL IT'S NOT FUN!

NOT FUN, NOT FUN, NOT FUN, NOT FUN, NOT FUN.
NOT FUN, NOT FUN, NOT FUN, NOT FUN, NOT FUN.
NOT FUN, NOT FUN, NOT FUN, NOT FUN, F—UN,
POVERTY'S NOT FUN!

SR. M. ANNETTE. What do you mean, poverty's not fun?
YOU CAN'T DENY WE LIVE LIKE WE'RE FROM
    BEVERLY HILLS
WHILE MOTHER SUPERIOR PAYS ALL THE BILLS!
WAKE UP, SMELL THE COFFEE, GIRL, OUR LIVES ARE
    FIRST-RATE!
FROM A NUN'S POINT OF VIEW, POVERTY'S GREAT!

SR. AMNESIA. What are you talking about, "poverty's great?"
SR. M. ANNETTE. Well, isn't it obvious? We can *have* everything. We just can't *own* it!
SR. AMNESIA. (*looking embarrassed*) Oh—
CHASTITY IS WHERE WE'VE FOUND
OUR POSTULANTS ARE LOSING GROUND.
YOU MUST BE CELIBATE,
SR. M. ANNETTE.
YOU CAN'T SCREW AROUND!
SR. AMNESIA. (*shocked*) Sister!
OBEDIENCE IS NUMBER THREE.
WE CANNOT QUESTION WHAT WILL BE.
IF YOU HAVE NO OPINIONS
THE LIVIN' IS EASY—
(*There is a musical figure reminiscent of "Summertime."*) Wait a minute. I think I'm beginning to remember who I am.
SR. M. ANNETTE. It was Gershwin, honey, 1935 and you weren't in it! Now back to obedience!
IF PAIN CAN MAKE YOU PERFECT THEN THIS VOW IS
    FOR YOU.
EVERY TIME YOU DISOBEY THEY BEAT YOUR ASS
    BLACK AND BLUE!
SR. AMNESIA. (*mortified*)
THE CONFESSIONAL'S WHERE SHE BELONGS.
EVERYTHING SHE SAYS IS WRONG.
SR. M. ANNETTE.
SISTER'S JUST JEALOUS CAUSE I STOLE HER SONG.

Sr. Amnesia.
DEDICATION AND COMMITMENT—
Sr. M. Annette.
YOU'RE SO FULL OF—
Sr. Amnesia.
DON'T FINISH THAT ONE!
Sr. M. Annette.
NO HABIT, NO TICKET TO FUN!
Sr. Amnesia. (*pointing her finger at SR. M. ANNETTE*)
THIS SONG IS—(*SR. M. ANNETTE bites SR. AMNESIA's finger.*)
Ouch!
Sr. M. Annette. Get the hook!
Sr. Amnesia.
DONE!

[MUSIC CUE 10A: NUN PLAYOFF]

(*SR. AMNESIA exits R. with puppet. REV. MOTHER jumps up from her seat.*)

Rev. Mother. Why didn't someone tell me she had her puppet? (*to SR. HUBERT*) *You* knew! I know *you* knew! (*SR. HUBERT starts chuckling.*) Now, what if we have some plain clothes nuns in our audience? (*to audience*) I certainly hope no one was offended!

Sr. Hubert. Please don't let this affect your generosity this evening.

Rev. Mother. Really. We've gotta get those girls outta the freezer. I mean, you never know when the Health Inspector might be coming around.

Sr. Amnesia. (*entering R. without puppet*) Did I miss something?

Rev. Mother. Just the boat, dear.

Sr. Amnesia. Oh, but Reverend Mother, we don't have a boat. Sister drove the car!

Sr. Leo. (*getting up from her stool*) Amnesia, Reverend Mother was just saying that she didn't know when the Health Inspector might be coming around.

Sr. Amnesia. Oh, he came this afternoon.

Rev. Mother. What do you mean?—"He came this afternoon." You've been here all day practicing with us.

Sr. Amnesia. Oh, but he called yesterday.

All but Sr. Amnesia. What?!! (*SR. HUBERT and SR. ROBERT ANNE jump up from the stools at the counter. They are obviously upset at hearing this.*)

Rev. Mother. Amnesia, why don't you tell me these things?

Sr. Amnesia and Rev. Mother. I forgot.

Rev. Mother. Oh, this is terrible. Amnesia, go and phone the convent right away and see if anything's happened.

(*SR. AMNESIA runs up the stairs to the phone to make the call. SR. LEO and SR. ROBERT ANNE move up toward the juke box, discussing the situation, inaudibly, as REV. MOTHER continues the scene with SR. HUBERT.*)

Rev. Mother. (*continued*) This is just awful. Lord only knows what may have happened. Sister Hubert, I thought I told you to see that she reports everything to me!

Sr. Hubert. Now, don't try to blame this one on me. You're the one who bought the *Beta-Max*!

Rev. Mother. Don't start with that. You know very well that I didn't realize there wasn't enough money.

[music cue 11: mock fifties]

(*SR. LEO and SR. ROBERT ANNE accidentally "start" the juke box and 50's music comes blaring out. This is actually played and sung by the conductor/band with SR. LEO and SR. ROBERT ANNE joining in the singing. SR. ROBERT ANNE grabs REV. MOTHER and starts doing the "Lindy" dance with her.*)

Sr. Robert Anne, Sr. Leo, and Conductor/Band.
SHA NA NA NA NA NA,
SHA NA NA NA NA NA,
SHA NA NA NA NA NA, NA!

Rev. Mother. Stop it! Turn that thing off! Stop it!

(*Music out. SR. AMNESIA comes hurrying down the stairs from the phone.*)

Sr. Amnesia. Reverend Mother, Reverend Mother, I got the answering machine.

REV. MOTHER. Yes—go on—

SR. AMNESIA. It said that Sister Ralph Marie had to go down to the Board of Health for questioning!

REV. MOTHER. Oh no—now you've done it, Amnesia. Now you've really done it. This is a fine mess you've gotten us into!

SR. AMNESIA. But, I didn't mean to. I'm sorry. I didn't mean to!

(*SR. AMNESIA starts to cry and runs off* R. *SR. ROBERT ANNE and SR. LEO follow her.*)

SR. HUBERT. Regina, you didn't have to be so hard on her.

REV. MOTHER. Oh, you know I didn't mean it. Go and see if she's alright.

(*SR. HUBERT exits* R. *REV. MOTHER moves* D.C.)

REV. MOTHER. (*continued; to audience:*) I tell ya, it's not easy being a Mother Superior these days—trying to be a leader in these permissive times is almost impossible.

Take Sister Robert Anne for example—when she entered the convent they told me she was streetwise. Now, I thought that meant she knew her way around town! This girl knows things you don't *see* on Cable Television!

Why just this morning she comes into my office and she tells me that she's writing a book for her gym class on feminine hygiene. Do you know what she's gonna call it? "The Catholic Girl's Guide to an Immaculate Conception."

I'm tellin' you it's *not* easy! Sometimes I wonder why I ever became a nun in the first place—I didn't *have* to! The other Sisters don't know this, but I started out to be a tightrope walker. I'm not makin' this up, ya know. My mother and father had a highwire act. They were billed as Two Tons on a Tightrope—our whole family's a bit on the hefty side. My father said if we worked real hard we could be better than the Flying Wallendas—all of us kids were in the act—well, all except Mary Claire—that's our sister—she took up with a contortionist and one night they were trying out a new position when—uh—oh, dear! Never mind, I was telling another story. I was telling you about the act. Anyway we got booked in London and we had a wire stretched across the river as a publicity stunt—no net, mind you! Well, Two Tons on a Tightrope were up there when the wire snapped and suddenly—BOOM—Two

Tons in the Thames! Right then and there I promised the Lord that
if He'd save them I'd become a nun. Well, how as I to know He was
gonna come through? I thought they were gonners for sure!! Well,
since the Lord kept His part of the bargain I figured I'd better keep
mine, so here I am.

But you wanna know the truth—(*very wistfully*)—now that
I'm here, I wouldn't have it any other way. Still, I gotta tell ya
something—

(*She points her finger to the spotlight operator. The spotlight
    comes on and the music starts.*)

[MUSIC CUE 12: "TURN UP THE SPOTLIGHT"]

REV. MOTHER.
I SEE THE SPOTLIGHT, AND THOUGH IT'S NOT RIGHT,
I SIMPLY CAN'T RESIST IT'S CALL.
FOR SOME NUNS IT'S BINGO AT THE PARISH HALL.
TURN UP THE SPOTLIGHT AND I HAVE A BALL!

I LOSE MY HEAD, THEN
I KNOW I'M DEAD WHEN
I START TO HEAR THAT LAUGHTER GROW.
PLEASE, FORGIVE ME, BUT DON'TCHA KNOW,
THIS IS MUCH MORE FUN THAN B-I-N-G-O . . .
OH—OH—

(*REV. MOTHER has moved upstage and up the stairs so she is
    standing on the platform facing the audience. An umbrella
    is tossed to her through the upstage doorway. She pops the
    umbrella open and finishes the song pretending to be walk-
    ing the tightrope.*)

TURN UP THAT SPOTLIGHT
CAUSE WHEN I'VE GOT LIGHT
I'M A BARREL FULL OF FUN.
I'M YOUR RIGHT REVEREND MAMA,
SAY, "HELLO, DALAI-LAMA!"

Oy vey!

I'M YOUR RIGHT REVEREND MOTHER,
THERE ISN'T ANY OTHER.
YOUR RIGHT REVEREND MOTHER,
SUPERIOR NUN. OH, YEAH!

[MUSIC CUE 12A: SPOTLIGHT PLAYOFF]

(*REV. MOTHER is doing a "strut" across the stage as SR. HUBERT and SR. AMNESIA enter* R. *applauding. Music out.*)

SR. HUBERT. Well, you're turning out to be a regular Sophie Tucker!

(*REV. MOTHER looks embarrassed, and hands the umbrella to SR. HUBERT. SR. HUBERT takes the umbrella and sticks it behind the counter as she and SR. AMNESIA move the counter platform* D.C.)

SR. AMNESIA. Was she a Mother Superior, too?
SR. HUBERT. Not quite, dear.

(*SR. AMNESIA takes a seat on the stool closest to* C.S. *SR. LEO enters* L. *carrying a bouquet of lilacs. Only SR. AMNESIA sees SR. LEO.*)

SR. AMNESIA. Lilacs!
SR. HUBERT. (*thinking SR. AMNESIA is now "seeing" things tries to humor her*) Alright.
REV. MOTHER. (*now seeing SR. LEO*) Lilacs!

[MUSIC CUE 13: "LILACS BRING BACK MEMORIES"]

(*SR. AMNESIA does a doubletake to the audience.*)

SR. HUBERT. How beautiful! Where'd they come from?
SR. LEO. There's a card.
REV. MOTHER. (*pulling the card from the flowers and opening it*) Why, they're from the Ladies' Altar Society wishing us "good luck."
SR. HUBERT. Wasn't that sweet of them!
SR. LEO. (*moves* D.L.) These sure bring back memories.

"LILACS BRING BACK MEMORIES"

EVERYTIME I SMELL LILACS
I REMEMBER MY FIRST ROMANCE.
I WAS PUTTING ON A BALLET IN MY BACKYARD
WHEN I FELL IN LOVE WITH THE DANCE.

SR. HUBERT. (*looking at SR. LEO holding the lilacs*) Everytime *I* smell lilacs —
I REMEMBER THAT VERY SPECIAL DAY
WHEN THE BISHOP CAME AND GAVE ME MY NEW
    NAME.

(*She looks at the ring on her hand.*) Hubert! I thought I was gonna die!

SR. LEO. (*very excitedly*) Wait a minute! Wait a minute! Amnesia, I've got an idea!
IF LILACS MAKE US REMEMBER THINGS
THAT HAPPENED LONG AGO,

ALL but SR. AMNESIA.
MAYBE THE FRAGRANCE CAN TAKE YOU
    BACKWARDS
IN TIME, TO A PLACE YOU KNOW.

(*SR. LEO hands the lilacs to SR. AMNESIA and she buries her face in them for a moment.*)

SR. AMNESIA.
THEY SMELL VERY NICE, IT'S TRUE.
BUT THEY DON'T REMIND ME OF ANYTHING.
WAIT A MINUTE — YES, THEY DO.

(*REV. MOTHER, SR. HUBERT, and SR. LEO with great expectations make a grand move behind SR. AMNESIA and sing.*)

REV. MOTHER, SR. LEO and SR. HUBERT.
THEY DO?!!!

SR. AMNESIA.
I'M RUNNING THROUGH THE FIELD WITH THE
    NEIGHBOR KIDS
AND I HEAR MAMA CALLING ME TO GO.
DINNER IS READY. HURRY HOME NOW.
BUT I CAN'T REMEMBER WHO.

REV. MOTHER, SR. LEO and SR. HUBERT. (*with great disappointment*) Oh, no!

[MUSIC CUE 14: THE WITCH]

(*There is an immediate musical seque from "Lilacs" into "The Witch." SR. ROBERT ANNE enters* U., *cackling loudly, and runs down the stairs and jumps on the Exercycle. She has put a large paper cup on top of her head, under her veil, creating the effect of a witch's hat.*)

SR. ROBERT ANNE. (*screeching*) I'll get you my pretty. And your mangy little dog, too!
REV. MOTHER. (*furious, runs up and pulls SR. ROBERT ANNE off the Exercycle*) Get down here, right now. What do you think you're doing? There are people out there!

(*SR. ROBERT ANNE is arguing with REV. MOTHER the entire time. The other Sisters also begin talking. SR. ROBERT ANNE gets everyone's attention when she says:*)

SR. ROBERT ANNE. Wait a minute! I have to tell you something important.
REV. MOTHER. Well, what is it?!
SR. ROBERT ANNE. When I was in the Girl's Locker Room fixing my veil I found *this*! (*She pulls a small brown paper bag out from under her scapular.*)
REV. MOTHER. (*taking the bag*) Well, what is it? Never mind, I'll take care of it.

(*Everyone starts asking, "what's in the bag?" Over the confusion REV. MOTHER shouts:*)

REV. MOTHER. (*continued*) Hubert, get them ready for the first act finale. Hurry up, all of you. Get ready for the first act finale.

(*SR. LEO, SR. ROBERT ANNE, SR. AMNESIA, and SR. HUBERT exit* R. *REV. MOTHER moves* D.C.)

REV. MOTHER. (*continued*) I'm terribly sorry for this delay, they'll only be a moment. Now what is this she's fussing about?

(*REV. MOTHER sits down at the counter stool closest to* c. *The spotlight fades up on her. She discovers a small bottle of liquid in the bag and holds it up. It contains a substance called "Rush" which, if inhaled, causes an almost instant "high" feeling. It, like airplane glue, etc., is the type of thing that today's students might be fooling around with, much to the chagrin of the nuns.*)

Well, it's called "Rush" — it must be something for people in a hurry — (*She examines the bottle.*) — I guess you take a spoonful after every meal — let's see — no — it says here: "Remove cap, allow to stand, aroma will develop." Aroma? What kind of aroma?

(*She opens the bottle and takes a whiff.*)

Oooohhh — Good Lord it smells awful. Why would anyone want this stuff? R U S — Oh! (*It has hit her. She puts her finger inside the edge of her headpiece as if to loosen it a bit — she starts to laugh.*)

Is it warm in here? I'm awfully warm — It must be the — (*She indicates her headpiece.*)

I don't know what the girls are doing with this stuff but it can't be good for you.

It smells just awful. (*She opens the bottle and takes another whiff. She's laughing much more now.*)

Is it hot in here? It must be the lights!

Alright, in a few monents, minents, moments (*hysterical laughter*) we'll get back to Nundance — No — FLASHNUN (*She flips her scapular as if to flash the audience — more hysterical laughter.*) — Butch Cassidy and the Sundance Nun — no, that's not right.

(*She turns to the band.*) What show is this? Never mind. I'm alright, I'm alright. (*to audience*) Okay, let's get back and watch a couple of butch nuns dance! (*pause*) Did I say that? Oh, that's not right. (*Laughter continues.*)

You know, this stuff is absolutely marvelous! I'm gonna take some of this back to the convent.

(*She holds one finger to the side of her nose while she takes a huge snort.*)

Whooooaaaaaaa!

Do you want to try this? (*She gets up and goes toward band.*)
Have you guys tried this? It's wonderful. (*She moves toward the audience.*) Have you tried it?
It's hot in here!! (*She falls to the floor, laughing hysterically.*)

(*SR. HUBERT followed by SR. LEO and SR. AMNESIA enter R. running to help REV. MOTHER. SR. HUBERT is wearing black tap shoes but does not call attention to this fact. She gets REV. MOTHER on her feet as she sings:*)

"TURN OFF THE SPOTLIGHT"

SR. HUBERT.
TURN OFF THAT

[MUSIC CUE 15: TURN OFF THE SPOTLIGHT]

SPOTLIGHT! (*Spotlight out.*)
REV. MOTHER.
WAIT I'M NOT QUITE—
SR. HUBERT.
YES, YOU ARE!

(*SR. HUBERT takes REV. MOTHER off R. as SR. LEO and SR. AMNESIA move the counter back to its original position.*)

SR. AMNESIA.
SHE'S STONED!
SR. LEO.
COULD YA DIE!
SR. ROBERT ANNE. (*enters R.*)
WHAT'S GOING ON?
SR. LEO.
REVEREND MOTHER GOT HIGH!
SR. ROBERT ANNE.
I COULDA TOLD HER THAT STUFF MAKES YOU FLY!
SR. AMNESIA.
YOU'RE GONNA FRY.
SR. ROBERT ANNE.
HEY, NOW I—didn't tell her to use it!

(*SR. HUBERT enters R. with a shopping bag full of tap shoes.*)

Sr. Hubert.
PUT ON THESE SHOES, C'MON ALL OF YOU.
THERE'S BEEN A SLIGHT CHANGE IN WHAT'S ABOUT
  TO ENSUE.
Sr. Robert Anne.
I THOUGHT WE PLANNED THIS SONG FOR ACT TWO!
Sr. Hubert.
WELL, WE DID. BUT IT'S NOT. WE'VE GOTTA DO IT.
  NOW!

(*A moment of raucous laughter from REV. MOTHER is heard offstage. SR. ROBERT ANNE takes the bag of tap shoes and exits* R. *along with SR. LEO and SR. AMNESIA. They put on the tap shoes offstage, while SR. HUBERT continues onstage.*)

[MUSIC CUE 16: "TACKLE THAT TEMPTATION WITH A TIME-STEP"]

Sr. Hubert. (*continued*)
IF EVER YOU ARE TEMPTED TO TRANSGRESS
REMEMBER THIS:
(*Another burst of laughter from REV. MOTHER is heard offstage.*)
AN IDLE MIND IS WHERE THE DEVIL WORKS,
SO IN MY ANALYSIS—
IF BUSY HANDS ARE HAPPY HANDS,
THEN DANCING FEET ARE BLISS! SO:

TACKLE THAT TEMPTATION WITH A TIME-STEP.
NOT A ONE-STEP OR A TWO-STEP, BUT A TIME-STEP.
(*SR. HUBERT starts tap dancing.*)
STOMP-HOP-SHUFFLE-STEP-FA-LAP-STEP-STOMP
IN YOUR TAP SHOES.
YOU CAN CHASE THE DEVIL OUT
AND SHOUT THE GOOD NEWS.
TACKLE THAT TEMPTATION WITH A TIME-STEP
BEFORE TEMPTATION TACKLES YOU!

I said:

(*SR. HUBERT Motions for others to join her. They enter* R. *singing and dancing.*)

ALL.
TACKLE THAT TEMPTATION WITH A TIME-STEP.
NOT A ONE-STEP OR A TWO-STEP, BUT A TIME-STEP.
AND IF THAT'S NOT ENOUGH, THEN GO
AND SHUFFLE OFF TO BUFFALO.
TACKLE THAT TEMPTATION WITH A TIME-STEP
BEFORE TEMPTATION TACKLES YOU!

(*There is a dance break here. When the flamenco section is played REV. MOTHER enters* U. *with the "Convent Miranda" fruit hanging from her veil. She comes down the stairs and crashes through the line of nuns.*)

SR. HUBERT. Reverend Mother! (*to the others*) Get her out of here. She's ruining my big number! (*The others try to push her back on the car seat as the song continues.*)
ALL but REV. MOTHER.
TURN UP THE SPOTLIGHT,
THOUGH THIS IS NOT QUITE
WHAT WE EXPECTED WE WOULD DO.
WE'RE GONNA TAKE A BREAK,
PLEASE, COME BACK FOR HEAVEN'S SAKE.
THERE'S A LOT MORE IN ACT TWO.
REV. MOTHER. (*sticking her head out between two nuns*)
Peek-a-boo!
ALL but REV. MOTHER.
UNTIL THEN—
REV. MOTHER. Toodle-oo!

(*All exit* R., *then REV. MOTHER tries to return as the spotlight picks her up. A nun yanks her off stage. Blackout.*)

End ACT ONE

ACT TWO

Towards the end of intermission, SR. LEO, SR. HUBERT, and SR. AMNESIA mingle in the audience. As the house lights go to half and the stage lights come up, SR. ROBERT ANNE enters R.

SR. ROBERT ANNE. Sister Hubert? Are you out there, Sister Hubert?

SR. HUBERT. Yes, what is it, Sister?

SR. ROBERT ANNE. I need to see you. Go on talking, folks. We'll be starting in just a few minutes.

(SR. HUBERT followed by SR. LEO and SR. AMNESIA comes onto the stage to confer with SR. ROBERT ANNE. The four of them "huddle" for a moment.)

SR. ROBERT ANNE. (*to audience*) We're having a little problem backstage. It's nothing serious. Reverend Mother just got a message and she has to talk to somebody important. What I'm trying to say is: The understudy is on! Hang on just a second. (*to the other nuns*) You can get ready for the next number and I'll handle everything here.

SR. HUBERT. Are you sure you're okay?

SR. ROBERT ANNE. Oh, yeah. No problem.

(SR. HUBERT exits R. SR. LEO and SR. AMNESIA exit L.)

SR. ROBERT ANNE. (*continued*) Alriiiight! Now that I have you alone for a few moments I'd like to share something with you that I think you'll get a kick out of. And that's some more of my "habit humor." Now, you're probably wondering what nuns do in their spare time. Well, this particular nun likes to create other nuns. For instance:

(She takes each side of her veil and pulls it forward over her shoulders. She begins twisting the veil into "braids" starting with the part closest to the head working on down to the ends. She stretches the braids long and straight.) Sister Pocahontas! How!

(She swags the braids.) Yodle-ay-he-hoo! Sister Heidi!

47

(*She lifts her right leg with the knee bent.*) Sister Pippi Long-
stockings!

(*She stretches the braids above her head.*) Atilla the Nun!! Oh,
here's one of my favorites.

(*She twists the braids around her ears ala Princess Leia in "Star
Wars."*) Help me, Obi Wan Kenobi. You are my only hope!
Okay, I got one more. This takes a little time so bear with me.
(*to CONDUCTOR*) How 'bout some mood music?

[MUSIC CUE 17: THE VEIL]

(*The following is spoken during the time it takes to create the
last impression, which is done by taking the "braids" and ty-
ing them in a double knot just above the forehead. The sides
are tucked into the roll of the braids creating the look of an
old-fashioned hairdo.*)

Tell me if you see anybody coming, okay? You know, sometimes I do these for my students. They think they're hysterical.
Of course, they love to laugh. That's how I get through to them,
you know, by being funny. I teach seventh grade. That is a
rough age to be. I oughta know. When I was in seventh grade, I
got sent to St. Clare's School for the Deplorable. Okay here we
go, the final impression of the evening.

(*She raises her head with appropriate tremor ala Katharine
Hepburn. The music segues.*)

[MUSIC CUE 17A: SPRING SONG]

The callalilies are in bloom again! Such a strange flower!

(*She bows and puts her veil back as it should be. Music out.*)

Let's not mention this to You-Know-Who. Reverend Mother
does not always appreciate my methods or my behavior. But ya
gotta understand. I grew up in Canarsie. You know where that
is? Brooklyn! Yo!! Mamma!! Scungili!! You had to be tough.
And I was. I was one tough kid.

(*She gets the stool from beside the juke box and brings it* D.C.
and sits down to tell her story.)

See, my dad was never around much and my mom had to
work two jobs and so us kids were alone a lot. I was always in
trouble — which is why I got sent to Saint Clare's. But, hey, it's
okay. Things have worked out. My background has even paid
off a little bit. Not only do I drive the convent car, but I can also
strip it faster than any mechanic in Hoboken! You know, a lot
of my old friends still cannot believe that I am a nun. But I have
to tell you why. It's all because of Sister Rose Francis.

[MUSIC CUE 18: "GROWING UP CATHOLIC"]

She was the head of Saint Clare's. Boy, oh boy, she was some-
thin' else. She was the one person who made me believe that I
was worth something. And I want to be just like her. Sometimes
I miss Saint Clare's. Things were really different back then. It
was a long time ago.

"GROWING UP CATHOLIC"

SR. ROBERT ANNE. (*continued*)
AT SAINT CLARE'S SCHOOL, RELIGION CLASS
BEGAN WITH MASS EACH DAY.
IT WAS SAID IN LATIN THEN.
THAT'S HOW I LEARNED TO PRAY.

THE NUNS APPEARED IN BLACK AND WHITE,
(*SR. HUBERT, SR. LEO, and SR. AMNESIA enter* U. *and
form a little "choir" on the stairs. They "ooh" as SR. ROB-
ERT ANNE continues singing.*)
AND SO DID EVERY RULE.
THINGS WERE EITHER WRONG OR RIGHT
AT SAINT CLARE'S CATHOLIC SCHOOL.

(*SR. ROBERT ANNE stands.*)

SR. HUBERT, SR. LEO and SR. AMNESIA.
HOSANNA!

ALL FOUR.
HOSANNA!
HOSANNA IN EXCELSIS.
EXCELSIS, IN EXCELSIS.
SR. ROBERT ANNE.
BUT THEN THE RULES BEGAN TO CHANGE
AND MANY LOST THEIR WAY.
WHAT WAS ALWAYS BLACK AND WHITE
WAS TURNING SHADES OF GRAY.

(*SR. HUBERT, SR. AMNESIA, and SR. LEO walk slowly down the stairs and stand in a diagonal line upstage and left of SR. ROBERT ANNE.*)

ALL FOUR.
HOLY, HOLY, HOLY,
HOLY LORD!
SR. ROBERT ANNE.
THOUGH MASS IS SAID IN ENGLISH NOW,
TO MAKE US MORE AWARE,
CONFUSION SEEMS TO REIGN SUPREME
LIKE GOD. IT'S EVERYWHERE.

(*SR. HUBERT, SR. LEO, and SR. AMNESIA sing "oohs" in the background.*)

THE CHURCH IS QUITE PROGRESSIVE NOW
THOUGH PEOPLE RIDICULE
THE FACT THAT SO MANY THINGS ARE OPTIONAL
IT'S HARD TO FIND A RULE.

THROUGH IT ALL I'VE OFTEN SAID
THOSE ANCIENT LATIN PRAYERS
THAT I FIRST LEARNED WHEN GROWING UP —
CATHOLIC — AT ST. CLARE'S.
SR. HUBERT, SR. LEO and SR. AMNESIA.
HOSANNA!
ALL FOUR.
HOSANNA!
HOSANNA IN EXCELSIS!
IN EXCELSIS, IN EXCELSIS,
IN EXCELSIS!

(*Lights fade out, then back up quickly.*)

(*SR. ROBERT ANNE has put the stool back and is telling the
    other Sisters what a lovely job they did singing when REV.
    MOTHER enters* R. *very excitedly. She is carrying a sum-
    mons.*)

SR. ROBERT ANNE. What's the matter with you?
REV. MOTHER. This summons just came. That's what's the
matter!
SR. ROBERT ANNE. Well, it can't be *that* bad. You should see
your face!

(*SR. ROBERT ANNE takes the summons as the others crowd
    around to look at it. There is an audible sound of shock!*)

[MUSIC CUE 19: "WE'VE GOT TO CLEAN OUT THE FREEZER"]

SR. ROBERT ANNE. (*continued*)
WE'VE GOT TO CLEAN OUT THE FREEZER
    SR. LEO.
BY TOMORROW MORNING.
    SR. AMNESIA and SR. HUBERT.
CAUSE THE JERSEY BOARD OF HEALTH
HAS SENT THE FINAL WARNING.
    ALL.
THEY'RE NOT BUYING OUR LINE
THAT DEAD NUNS RISE AND SHINE.
WE MUST COMPLY OR FACE A FINE!

(*The next section is very soft, but intense:*)

WE'VE GOT TO CLEAN OUT THE FREEZER
CAUSE THEY KNOW WE'RE THE ONES
WHO HAVE REFUSED TO START DEFROSTING
THOSE FOUR BLUE NUNS!
THE TIME HAS COME TO SEND THEM OFF
TO THEIR REWARD
AND LET THEM GREET THE LORD!

(*Full voice:*)

HEAVEN AWAITS!

SO PACK 'EM IN CRATES
AND TELL SAINT PETER
THEY'LL BE AT THOSE PEARLY GATES.
AND TELL HIM THESE ARE NUNS ON ICE
THAT WE ARE CERTAIN DIDN'T SIN,
AND WE'D BE VERY GRATEFUL
IF HE'D LET 'EM COME IN.

WE'VE GOT TO CLEAN OUT THE FREEZER
BY TOMORROW MORNIN'.
SOMEONE HOLLER TO GABRIEL
TO BLOW HIS HORN 'N'
WHEN THE SAINTS GO MARCHING
TO THAT HEAV'NLY DOOR
TELL 'EM THERE'S GONNA BE FOUR MORE!

WE'VE GOT TO CLEAN OUT THE FREEZER
AND DEFROST THE DEAD.
BECAUSE THE JERSEY BOARD OF HEALTH
IS CLAIMING THEY WERE MISLED.
THEY'RE NOT BUYING OUR LINE
THAT DEAD NUNS RISE AND SHINE.
WE MUST BURY THEM INSTEAD.
THEY'RE NOT BUYING OUR LINE—
NUNS RISE AND SHINE—
WE MUST BURY THEM INSTEAD!

They're dead!

(*The phone begins to ring. SR. ROBERT ANNE, SR. AM-
NESIA, and SR. LEO all begin to holler, "I'll get it!" and
race up the steps to the phone. REV. MOTHER is obviously
frustrated by their behavior, but realizes that someone has
to answer the phone.*)

SR. LEO. I'll get it. I'm younger. (*The others look at each other
as if to say, "What has that got to do with it?" SR. LEO picks up
the phone.*) Hello. Mount Saint Helen's.
    REV. MOTHER. Well, who is it, Leo?
    SR. LEO. Sister Mary Euthanasia!
    ALL. Our nurse!

[MUSIC CUE 20: EUTHANASIA'S CHORD]

(*The lights flicker ala "grade B horror movie."*)

SR. LEO. She says Sister Julia—Child of God (*All cross themselves.*), was trying out a new Chinese Dish—Chicken with Feenamints—or something like that—anyway, it backfired and she's in the hospital getting her stomach pumped!

REV. MOTHER. Oh, Lord deliver me — is she coming over to do the show?

SR. LEO. (*into phone*) Is she coming over to do the show? (*to REV. MOTHER*) No!

REV. MOTHER. No?

SR. LEO. No! (*SR. LEO hangs up phone.*)

REV. MOTHER. Whoa!

SR. ROBERT ANNE. Oh! I can do my number!

REV. MOTHER and SR. HUBERT. I don't think so.

(*SR. LEO has hung up the phone and all the nuns come D.C.*)

REV. MOTHER. Well, I'll just have to fill in for Sister Julia. Now let's see — I'll need her book — does anyone know what happened to her book?

SR. AMNESIA. Oh, I forgot to bring it in! I left it in the station wagon.

REV. MOTHER. Well, I've got to have that book. Will one of you get it, please?

SR, AMNESIA, SR. ROBERT ANNE and SR. LEO. I will!

REV. MOTHER. Alright, all three of you go.

SR. AMNESIA. You know what I like best about this show?

ALL but SR. AMNESIA. What?

SR. AMNESIA. We haven't had to stoop to a single penguin joke! (*Looking directly at REV. MOTHER she points her index fingers to the floor and does the "punctuation gesture."*)

[MUSIC CUE 21: PENGUIN WALK]

(*SR. AMNESIA exits R. SR. LEO and SR. ROBERT ANNE follow her and start walking like penguins, then when REV. MOTHER isn't looking SR. ROBERT ANNE grabs SR. LEO and they run up the stairs and out the upstage exit. Music segues.*)

[MUSIC CUE 22: JUST A COUPL'A SISTERS]

REV. MOTHER. Is this a test? Mother said there'd be days like this!

"JUST A COUPL'A SISTERS"

MANY PEOPLE THINK THAT IN A CONVENT
A REVEREND MOTHER'S SOMETHING LIKE A QUEEN.
NOTHING COULD BE FURTHER FROM THE TRUTH
  HERE.
(*to SR. HUBERT*)
SHALL WE SHOW THEM WHAT I MEAN?

SR. HUBERT. Whatever you say, Your Highness! (*REV. MOTHER gives a look to SR. HUBERT as if to say "very funny!"*)

REV. MOTHER. (*to CONDUCTOR*) Hit it!

BOTH.
WE'RE JUST A COUPL'A SISTERS
PLAIN AS WE CAN BE,
JUST A COUPL'A SISTERS
WHO'VE DISCOVERED HARMONY.

REV. MOTHER.
OH, SURE I COULD GO SOLO.

SR. HUBERT.
GOING SOLO CAN BE FUN.

BOTH.
BUT WHEN TWO SOLOS GET TOGETHER
THEY HARMONIZE AS ONE—NUN—
WE'RE JUST A COUPL'A SISTERS
OUT HERE HAVING FUN.

REV. MOTHER. (*pointing to SR. HUBERT*)
THE MISTRESS OF THE NOVICES,

SR. HUBERT. (*pointing to REV. MOTHER*)
AND REVEREND NUMBER ONE!

REV. MOTHER.
IT'S TRUE I AM IN CHARGE HERE
BUT I KNOW I'M NOT ALONE
AS LONG AS SISTER HUBERT
ADDS HER HARMONIZING TONE.

SR. HUBERT.
I TRAIN ALL OUR NOVICES
AND DO IT ON MY OWN.
CAUSE I KNOW REVEREND MOTHER'S NEAR—
A STEPPING STONE.

REV. MOTHER.
A stepping stone? A stepping stone to what, Hubert?

SR. HUBERT. Oh, Regina, it was just a rhyme. You see, the only other word I could think of was *overgrown* and I know how sensitive you are about your weight.

REV. MOTHER. Hubert, I'll have you know I am not fat! I'm just a little beefy!

SR. HUBERT. Ladies and gentlemen—The Whopper! (*REV. MOTHER glares at SR. HUBERT.*)

BOTH.
PUT US BOTH TOGETHER
AND WE'VE GOT IT ALL.

REV. MOTHER.
THE MELODY,

SR. HUBERT.
THE HARMONY,

BOTH.
SAINT PETER AND SAINT PAUL.

SR. HUBERT.
ALL WE NEED IS MARY
THEN WE'D HAVE A SINGING GROUP.

REV. MOTHER.
EVERY TOM AND DICK AND HARRY
IS A MARY IN THIS TROUPE!
Sister Mary Thomas,

SR. HUBERT.
Sister Mary Richard,

REV. MOTHER.
Sister Mary Harold,

SR. HUBERT.
Sister Maryknoll.

BOTH.
Sister Mary Martin, Sister Mary Pickford,
Sister Mary Sunshine, hey, we're on a roll.
Sister Mary Hartman, Sister Mary Astor,

SR. HUBERT.
Sister Merry Widow,

REV. MOTHER.
Sister, that's a wrap.

SR. HUBERT.
Sister Mary Poppins, Sister Merry Christmas.

REV. MOTHER.
Sister, that's enough of this "Mary" crap!

BOTH.
WE'RE JUST A COUPL'A SISTERS
IN WHAT YOU'D CALL "RARE FORM"
WHO'VE COME TO ENTERTAIN YOU
BY SINGING UP A STORM.
SWANEE, HOW I LOVE YA,
    SR. HUBERT.
I LOVE REVEREND MAMMY!
    BOTH.
WE'RE JUST A COUPL'A SISTERS,
PLAIN AS WE CAN BE.
JUST A COUPL'A SISTERS
WHO'VE DISCOVERED HARMONY!

(*SR. HUBERT and REV. MOTHER exit* R. *and return immediately during applause. SR. AMNESIA is behind them carrying the cookbook, bowl, whisk, egg carton, spoon, and wooden stand which she places on top of the counter. A second later SR. ROBERT ANNE enters* U. *and appears at the top of the stairs.*)

REV. MOTHER. (*to audience*) And now, ladies and gentlemen—
    SR. ROBERT ANNE. (*interrupting*) Presenting—The Dying Nun!

[MUSIC CUE 23: SOUP'S ON]

(*SR. ROBERT ANNE runs down the stairs and exits* L.)

"SOUP'S ON—THE DYING NUN BALLET"

(*SR. LEO enters* U. *and appears at the top of the stairs wearing a Sisters of Charity "Flying Nun" hat. SR. LEO does a lively dance on pointe during which SR. ROBERT ANNE enters* L. *carrying a soup tureen and ladle. She is wearing a chef's hat. She dances up to SR. LEO and gives her a spoonful of soup. SR. ROBERT ANNE then exits* L. *SR. LEO proceeds to "die" ala "The Dying Swan," using the "wings" of the hat as the wings of the swan. During the dance REV. MOTHER has sat down on the bed while SR. HUBERT has joined SR. AMNESIA at the counter. At the end of the dance SR.*

ROBERT ANNE enters L. *applauding. REV. MOTHER rises from the bed.*)

REV. MOTHER. Sister!!!

SR. LEO. Robert said you'd think it was *funny.*

REV. MOTHER. Robert, I've about had it with you. One more time and *you'll* be the "dying nun!" (*REV. MOTHER grabs the chef's hat off SR. ROBERT ANNE's head.*) Now get her outta that thing!

SR. LEO. It was just a joke.

REV. MOTHER. Well, it's not funny. Who do you think you are, Sally Field?

(*SR. LEO exits* L. *with SR. ROBERT ANNE. As REV. MOTHER turns back* C., *she sees SR. HUBERT imitating SR. LEO's dance.*)

REV. MOTHER. Hubert! Stop that. She'll see you.

SR. HUBERT. Well, it *was* pretty funny.

REV. MOTHER. It wasn't. It's not enough that I've got to contend with Sister Robert Anne. Now she's corrupting the novices.

(*During the next few lines the Sisters move the counter* C. *and put on the aprons which are stowed on a shelf in the rear of the counter. REV. MOTHER puts on the chef's hat.*)

SR. HUBERT. Oh, she's not so bad. At least she's not in jail!

SR. AMNESIA. Was Sister Robert Anne in jail?

REV. MOTHER. Well, Sing Sing wasn't the name of her giant panda!

SR. AMNESIA. Does she have a panda?

SR. HUBERT. Now, Reverend Mother, let's be fair — everybody who was anybody was in jail in the sixties.

REV. MOTHER. Well, it's not worth talking about. Besides, there is something much more exciting to discuss. And I'm talking about the publication of this book — (*She indicates the book on the counter.*) Baking with the B.V.M."

SR. HUBERT. Reverend Mother, I think since some of the people in our audience may have brought non-Catholic friends you should explain that the B.V.M. is the Blessed Virgin Mary.

REV. MOTHER. I was just getting to that, Hubert. "Baking with the *Blessed Virgin Mary*!" (*REV. MOTHER turns to SR.*

HUBERT and, with index fingers extended, they both do the "punctuation gesture.")—by our own Sister Julia—Child of God. (*All cross themselves.*) Well, now folks, first of all, the book has a beautiful cover featuring a picture of our Blessed Mother in her cook's hat and apron. Wait till you see this. You're gonna love it. (*She shows the audience the cover of the book.*) So you see, when you're not using it for baking it makes a lovely devotional addition to your kitchen.

Now, Sister Amnesia here has designed a terrific wooden stand for the book. (*REV. MOTHER sets up the stand and suddenly realizes that it is all crooked. After a doubletake she looks at SR. AMNESIA.*) Did you make that? (*SR. AMNESIA nods yes and grins.*) (*As an aside to SR. HUBERT*) She made that. (*REV. MOTHER looks back at SR. AMNESIA*) All by yourself? (*SR. AMNESIA nods yes and grins.*) (*As an aside to SR. HUBERT*) All by herself. (*REV. MOTHER looks back at SR. AMNESIA and then to SR. HUBERT*) Nice house—

BOTH. Nobody home!

(*REV. MOTHER turns the bookstand over, pushes it aside, smiles at SR. AMNESIA and continues.*)

REV. MOTHER. Many of our parishioners say this book is perfect for the top of the microwave. How comforting it is to have our Blessed Lady sitting on your Lean Cuisine. Well, shall we take a look at the book, Sisters?

(*All agree, yes.*)

I can see that the Main Section is just chock full of unusual recipes, especially suited for the Catholic Kitchen. For example: Here's Cesar Franck's Panis Angelicus—a delightful taste treat consisting of two hot dogs, wrapped in anchovies, and served on a slice of Wonder bread!!?? Has anybody ever tested this stuff?

SR. HUBERT. Why, no—we only saw the book today. We thought you went over all this with Julia.

REV. MOTHER. I went over it? Well, I thought you—(*The two begin arguing over who's responsibility it was, when REV. MOTHER stops the discussion by saying:*) Well, it's too late now, isn't it?

SR. HUBERT. In a word, yes!

REV. MOTHER. Well, we'll just go on! Now look at this—the mortally sinful devil's food cake.

SR. AMNESIA. Isn't that cute.

SR. HUBERT. Here's one. Mary Magdalene Tarts!

SR. AMNESIA. Oh! Here's a recipe for Girl Scouts.

REV. MOTHER. Why don't you read that one, Sister?

SR. AMNESIA. Okay. It says: First, get twelve brownies real hot!

(*REV. MOTHER and SR. HUBERT look at each other, shocked. REV. MOTHER slowly rips the page out of the cookbook and tosses it on the shelf under the counter, all the while smiling at the audience.*)

REV. MOTHER. It's a misprint. Moving right along—here's an interesting section: Historic Recipes. Look at this—Barbecued Ribs Saint Joan.

SR. HUBERT. Read this. Leg of Lamb of God!

REV. MOTHER. (*pause*) Oh my goodness, it says here that this is the recipe for the hors d'oerves served at the Last Supper—Host Toasties! (*They all laugh loudly.*) It serves thirteen! (*They laugh even louder.*)

SR. AMNESIA. Oh, that Julia. She's a real killer! (*REV. MOTHER and SR. HUBERT look in horror at SR. AMNESIA who immediately realizes what she has said.*)

REV. MOTHER. Well, the book is so loaded with mouth-watering treats I just can't decide what recipe we ought to try. (*She continues thumbing through the book.*)

SR. HUBERT. (*to audience*) You know, the book will be available after the program this evening and I'm sure you'll all want to get your own personal copy.

SR. AMNESIA. And Sister Julia has asked that all the profits from the book go to the burial fund.

REV. MOTHER. *Holy smoke!!*

(*SR. ROBERT ANNE and SR. LEO enter L. and rush to REV. MOTHER.*)

SR. ROBERT ANNE. What's the matter? Is something burning?

REV. MOTHER. No, she's included the recipe for that soup!

ALL. What?!!

REV. MOTHER. Look, it's right here—Vichychoisse Soup!

SR. HUBERT. Well, the recipe isn't poison, is it?

REV. MOTHER. How should I know? I should have known better than to trust that nitwit! Well, we certainly can't sell this thing!

SR. HUBERT. Well, what are we going to do? We were counting on the books to bring in some extra money.

[MUSIC CUE 24: SECOND FIDDLE REPRISE]

SR. AMNESIA. I could do my tongue percussion.

SR. LEO. And I could do my fire baton.

SR. HUBERT. No fire baton!

REV. MOTHER. And what, may I ask, is tongue percussion?

(*There is total chaos as ALL argue over what they are going to do. Above all this we hear:*)

SR. ROBERT ANNE. Oh, I don't believe this!

REV. MOTHER. What?

"PLAYING SECOND FIDDLE REPRISE"

SISTER ROBERT ANNE.
I'M CAUGHT IN THE MIDDLE
STILL PLAYING SECOND FIDDLE
WHILE YOU PEDDLE POISON RECIPES.
YOU COMPLETELY DISREGARD
THAT I'VE WORKED VERY HARD
ON A SONG—

REV. MOTHER. Well, sing it Louise!

SR. ROBERT ANNE. Do you really mean it?

(*SR. HUBERT, SR. AMNESIA, and SR. LEO put the counter back in its original position.*)

REV. MOTHER. Yes! Now get over there (*She indicates* C.) before I change my mind. Good Lord, I feel like I'm back in the Leper Colony the way things are falling to pieces here.

(*SR. ROBERT ANNE goes up to the band to be sure everything is set. REV. MOTHER and the OTHERS take the cookbook and utensils and exit* R. *As they are leaving we hear:*)

SR. HUBERT. How could Julia be so stupid!

REV. MOTHER. How could I be so stupid?

SR. HUBERT. Let me count the ways.

(*SR. ROBERT ANNE moves* D.C. *and music segues.*)

[MUSIC CUE 25: "I JUST WANT TO BE A STAR"]

SR. ROBERT ANNE.
WHEN I BECAME A NUN

AT A VERY EARLY AGE,
I HAD TO CHOOSE BETWEEN THE CONVENT
AND A LIFE UPON THE STAGE.
SO WHEN REVEREND MOTHER SAID,
"WE'RE PUTTIN' ON A SHOW,"
I MUST TELL YOU, I WAS THRILLED TO DEATH.
I COULDN'T WAIT TO GO.

WELL, NOW TO MY SURPRISE,
REVEREND MOTHER DIDN'T SEE
WHAT'S SO OBVIOUS.
THE STAGE IS MEANT FOR ME.
MONEY AND FAME,
I DON'T DESIRE.
I ONLY WANT TO SPARKLE.
I'M NOT HERE TO START A FIRE!

I DON'T CARE IF I'M EVER RICH OR FAMOUS,
I JUST WANT TO BE A STAR.
I DON'T CARE IF YOU KNOW WHAT MY NAME IS,
I JUST WANT TO BE A STAR.

I WANT TO BE
THE NUN WHO MAKES YOU CHEER.
THE NUN WHO'S OUT IN FRONT,
INSTEAD OF AT THE REAR.
FOR ONCE, I WANT
TO LEAD THE BAND
AND HAVE THE CROWD
IN THE PALM OF MY HAND.

I DON'T CARE IF I'M EVER RICH OR FAMOUS.
JUST SO I CAN BE A STAR!

WHEN WE BEGAN THIS SHOW,
THEY WERE REALLY GREEN.
THEY DIDN'T KNOW A CHORUS LINE
FROM A CHORUS QUEEN.
THEY DIDN'T REALIZE
THAT IN THE CHORUS LINE
YOU NEVER GET TO STRUT YOUR STUFF,
YOU NEVER REALLY SHINE!

I DON'T CARE IF I'M EVER RICH OR FAMOUS,
I JUST WANT TO BE A STAR.
SURE, IT'S TRUE THAT MY ONLY CLAIM TO FAME IS,
"I GOT WHAT IT TAKES TO BE A STAR!"

I KNOW MY VOW OF POVERTY
SAYS I CAN'T MAKE A FORTUNE,
BUT WHEN WE'RE EIGHTY
AND SETTIN' ON THE PORCH IN
THE OLD NUNS' HOME,
AND THEY ASK WHO WE ARE,
I JUST WANNA SAY,
"HEY! I WAS A STAR!"

I DON'T CARE IF I'M EVER RICH OR FAMOUS,
JUST SO I CAN BE—
THE CHORUS LINE IS NOT FOR ME—
I'M RED HOT TO BE A STAR.
HEY! REGINA, PARK YOUR OWN DAMN CAR!
I JUST WANNA BE A STAR!

[MUSIC CUE 25A: STAR PLAYOFF]

(*SR. ROBERT ANNE is acknowledging the applause, strutting across the stage. She is unaware of the fact that REV. MOTHER followed by SR. LEO and SR. AMNESIA have entered* R. *SR. ROBERT ANNE backs into REV. MOTHER. Music out.*)

Rev. Mother. Well, our little sparkler turned out to be quite a firecracker!

Sr. Robert Anne. I'm sorry, Reverend Mother.

Rev. Mother. Well, that certainly was a surprise, Robert. You were sensational!

Sr. Robert Anne. I was?

Rev. Mother. Yes, you were. That'll be six "Our Fathers" and seven hundred "Hail Marys." Now, get over there. (*She indicates* D.C.) Come on, all of you. (*SR. AMNESIA, SR. LEO and SR. ROBERT ANNE move* D.C. *REV. MOTHER is stage left of them.*) Ladies and gentlemen, we'd like to present our version of Patty, Maxine and Laverne—The Saint Andrews Sisters of Hoboken in a number they've created especially for this evening. Sisters—

(*REV. MOTHER exits* R. *SR. ROBERT ANNE nods to the*
   CONDUCTOR.)

[MUSIC CUE 26: "THE DRIVE-IN"]

ALL THREE.
IT SEEMS LIKE ONLY YESTERDAY
WHEN LIFE WAS QUITE SERENE.
THE DAYS WERE RATHER UNEVENTFUL,
WHAT YOU'D CALL ROUTINE.

THEN CAME THAT FATAL NIGHT
WHEN JULIA MADE HER VICHYSOISSE,
FOR FIFTY-TWO, "BON APPETIT"
WAS ALSO "BON VOYAGE."

THEN OUR TRANQUIL LIFE WAS OVER
FOR WE KNEW WHAT WE MUST DO.
WE HAD TO RAISE THE MONEY
TO INTER THE FIFTY-TWO!

AT TIMES IT ALL SEEMED HOPELESS
AND MUCH MORE THAN WE COULD BEAR.
WE WOULD ALL HAVE LOST OUR MINDS
HAD WE NOT STOPPED—
   SR. ROBERT ANNE.
TO GO TO THE DRIVE-IN,
   SR. AMNESIA.
AT THE SKYLINE DRIVE-IN,
   SR. LEO and SR. ROBERT ANNE.
DRIVE-IN,
   SR. LEO.
WE CAN ALWAYS SURVIVE IN,
   SR. AMNESIA and SR. ROBERT ANNE.
WE SURVIVE IN,
   ALL THREE.
TIMES OF STRESS AND STRAIN.
CAUSE FANTASIES THRIVE IN
   SR. AMNESIA.
THE SKYLINE DRIVE-IN,
   SR. LEO and SR. ROBERT ANNE.
DRIVE-IN.

SR. LEO.
IT'S THE ONE PLACE I'VE BEEN,
  SR. AMNESIA and SR. ROBERT ANNE.
ONE PLACE I'VE BEEN,
  ALL THREE.
THAT'LL ALWAYS EASE THE PAIN.

(*During the next section all three move up to the car seat. SR.
   LEO sits down in the middle as SR. AMNESIA and SR.
   ROBERT ANNE pull the wagon holding the seat D.C.*)

GIVE YOURSELF A CHANGE OF SCENE
BY ALTERING THE DAY'S ROUTINE.
FIND THE NEAREST MOVIE SCREEN
AND LET YOURSELF GO.

IT'S BETTER THAN A MAGAZINE,
OF COURSE, YOU'LL WANT TO KEEP IT CLEAN.
BUT IF IT'S A BIT OBSCENE
WHO'LL EVER KNOW?

THAT YOU'VE BEEN TO THE

(*During the next section SR. AMNESIA and SR. ROBERT
   ANNE, moving in 'slow motion,' rotate the 'wagon' 180
   degrees. The rear of the seat is the back end of the car
   "Greased Light'ning." Once the car is in position SR. AM-
   NESIA and SR. ROBERT ANNE also climb into the seats.
   The view becomes three nuns leaning over the backseat of
   the car as they continue the song.*)

DRIVE-IN.
HEY, WHEN YOU ARRIVE,
FIND A PLACE TO PARK AND DIVE IN
TO A BOX OF BUTTERED POPCORN
AND REVIVE YOURSELF.
YOUR SPIRITS COME ALIVE WHEN
YOU DON'T HAVE TO CONNIVE.
THERE ISN'T A RIVAL
WHEN A DRIVE'LL MEAN SURVIVAL
  SR. LEO.
AS SOON AS YOU ARRIVE IN,

Sr. Amnesia and Sr. Robert Anne.
YOU ARRIVE IN,
   Sr. Amnesia.
THE SKYLINE DRIVE-IN,
   Sr. Leo and Sr. Robert Anne.
DRIVE-IN.
   Sr. Amnesia.
IT'S THE ONE PLACE I'VE BEEN,
   Sr. Leo and Sr. Robert Anne.
ONE PLACE I'VE BEEN
   All Three.
THAT'LL CHASE THE BLUES AWAY.
(*They sigh.*)

ENOUGH BALLYHOO ABOUT WHAT TO DO.
IT'S TIME TO ROLL OUR HOMEMADE CONVENT FILM
   DISPLAY.
SCIDDLY-AH-DOO-BEE-DOO-WAH!

[MUSIC CUE 27: NUNSMOKE]

"NUNSMOKE"

(*The lights go down as a movie screen is lowered into place. If a portable screen is used it can be brought out by SR. HU-BERT. SR. LEO, SR. AMNESIA and SR. ROBERT ANNE sit down in the car seat. REV. MOTHER and SR. HUBERT enter* r. *and sit on the stools at the counter. The home "movie" Nunsmoke is shown. This is actually a slide show with pictures and silent film captions. During the "movie" a picture appears of REV. MOTHER in a bathing suit complete with headpiece, veil and rosary. She is outraged. She knows that SR. ROBERT ANNE and SR. LEO did this as they are laughing hysterically.*)

Rev. Mother. Stop it! Stop it!! Shut that off!!! Turn the lights on!

(*Music out. The screen is pulled back up, or if a portable screen is used, SR. HUBERT takes it off* r.)

Rev. Mother. (*continued*) You two! (*She indicates SR. LEO and SR. ROBERT ANNE.*) You did it! Come with me! I have never been so mortified! Where did you get that picture?

(*REV. MOTHER hauls the two of them out of the car seat and drags them off* R. *If SR. HUBERT did not remove the screen she exits with them. Just before they are offstage we hear:*)

SR. LEO. (*to audience*) Could ya die!

SR. AMNESIA. (*After a moment of silence SR. AMNESIA sticks her head up over the back of the car.*) I don't think this was supposed to happen. (*She pushes the car back up under the hair dryers, this time with the rear of the car facing the audience. She goes to confer with the CONDUCTOR.*) I don't think this was supposed to happen.

CONDUCTOR. I know.

SR. AMNESIA. Well, so what do I do now?

CONDUCTOR. Why don't you tell 'em one of your stories.

SR. AMNESIA. Oh, they don't want to hear one of my stories.

CONDUCTOR. Sure, they do.

SR. AMNESIA. You think so? Do you remember that story I was telling you last week?

CONDUCTOR. Yeah, that was a good one. Do *you* remember it?

SR. AMNESIA. Yeah, I think so. (*She turns to the audience.*) Okay! I'm gonna tell you a story. It's about me.

[MUSIC CUE 28: "I COULD'VE GONE TO NASHVILLE"]

(*SR. AMNESIA moves the bed downstage and then lies down on her back. Looking directly at the ceiling, she sings.*)

"I COULD'VE GONE TO NASHVILLE"

SR. AMNESIA.
SOMETIMES IN THE MORNING
BEFORE THE FIRST BELL RINGS,
I LIE HERE WIDE AWAKE
WONDERIN' ALL KINDS OF THINGS.

(*She sits bolt upright.*)

LIKE WHO I AM, OR WHAT I'D BE

IF I WERE NOT A NUN.
I SUPPOSE I COULD BE ANYTHING
BUT IF I COULD BE ANYONE—

(*She stands up beside the bed.*)

I'D LIKE TO BE A COUNTRY SINGER
LIKE LORETTA LYNN.
WITH A DELUXE WINNEBAGO
THAT I COULD TRAVEL IN.

I'D HAVE WIGS LIKE DOLLY PARTON.
I MIGHT EVEN PIERCE MY EARS.
I'D HAVE RHINESTONE STUDDED COWBOY BOOTS
AND A SEQUINED GOWN FROM SEARS.

I'd have me some back up singers.

(*We hear "back-up" oohing for a moment offstage.*)

And a real live bluegrass band.
AND I WOULD GO TO NASHVILLE
AND APPEAR AT OPRYLAND!

I'D SING SONGS OF INSPIRATION.
I'D SING SONGS IN TIME OF STRIFE.
SONGS LIKE "DROP-KICK ME, JESUS,
THROUGH THE GOAL POST OF LIFE!"

Wait a minute—wait a minute—it's all coming back to me—I
was going to be a country singer and there was a contest—a big
contest—and I remember walking out on this huge stage—(*She
moves* D.C. *as the spotlight hits her.*)

AND WHEN THEY TURNED UP THAT SPOTLIGHT
ALL THAT GLITTERED THERE WAS ME.
PEOPLE ALL WERE SAYING,
"SHE'S ANOTHER BRENDA LEE!"

OH, I COULD'VE GONE TO NASHVILLE
AND BECOME A COUNTRY STAR.
BUT SOMETHING DEEP INSIDE OF ME
WAS CALLING FROM AFAR.

(*She moves back over near the bed.*)

I STARTED MY NEW LIFE
INSIDE THE CONVENT WALL.
BRENDA LEE HAD GIVEN WAY
TO SISTER MARY — (*She pauses.*) — Paul —

Sister Mary Paul — Sister Mary Paul — (*She jumps on the bed with excitement.*) That's it! I'm Sister Mary Paul!

I REMEMBER IT ALL —

OH, I COULD'VE GONE TO NASHVILLE
AND BECOME LORETTA LYNN.
BUT SOMETHING MUCH MORE POWERFUL
WAS CALLING FROM WITHIN.

OH, I COULD'VE GONE TO NASHVILLE
BUT I CAME HERE THAT DAY.

(*She kneels on bed. All the lights go down except for a spotlight on her face.*)

I MUST SAY A LITTLE THANK-YOU PRAYER
THAT IT ALL TURNED OUT THIS WAY — Amen. (*Blackout*)

[MUSIC CUE 28A: NASHVILLE PLAYOFF]

(*The lights come back up and SR. AMNESIA is jumping on the bed.*)

SR. AMNESIA. Come out here, everybody! Come out here, hurry! I remember who I am!

(*REV. MOTHER, SR. LEO, SR. ROBERT ANNE, and SR. HUBERT come running on so fast that when REV. MOTHER stops they all run into each other.*)

SR. AMNESIA. (*continued*) I remember who I am! I was going to be a country singer and I was going to Nashville but I felt I had this calling and so I decided not to become a big star and I became unimportant like all of you! I'm Sister Mary Paul!

SR. LEO. Sister Mary Paul—that's a nice name, isn't it, Hubert?

(*REV. MOTHER helps SR. AMNESIA off the bed and motions to SR. LEO to put the bed back in its original position.*)

REV. MOTHER. You know, I remember hearing about a Sister Mary Paul when we were in France, but when we came back here no one knew what happened to her—and then you mysteriously appeared and all you could tell us was a crucifix fell on your head—so you're Sister Mary Paul! (*aside to SR. HUBERT*) Well, I guess that ends the hope that she's a Franciscan.

SR. ROBERT ANNE. (*to SR. AMNESIA*) Do you remember everything?

SR. AMNESIA. Well, I—yes—I think I do. You see, I won this contest and I had this chance to go to Nashville—and then I don't know—somehow I was drawn to becoming a nun. I'm sure it was the same way you all felt.

REV. MOTHER. (*Before the above speech is finished, REV. MOTHER interrupts.*) Oh, my heavens!

ALL but REV. MOTHER. What?!

REV. MOTHER. Sister Mary Paul was the name of the nun who won the Publishers' Clearing House Sweepstakes and they could never find her. (*to SR. AMNESIA*) That's you! (*All the nuns begin jumping for joy and screaming, ending with:*) Saints be praised! We're rich!

[MUSIC CUE 29: "GLORIA IN EXCELSIS DEO"]
ALL.
GLORIA IN EXCELSIS DEO!

SR. HUBERT. Somebody call Ed McMahon!

SR. LEO. This means we can bury the last four dead sisters!

SR. ROBERT ANNE. And we can get a 36-inch screen for the Beta-Max!

SR. AMNESIA. And I helped!

REV. MOTHER. You know, I was really starting to get worried about having to defrost those girls tomorrow morning. I mean, Jersey smells bad enough as it is!

SR. HUBERT. It just goes to show that the Lord does, indeed, work in mysterious ways.

SR. ROBERT ANNE. One minute we're desperate—

SR. AMNESIA. The next minute, we're rich!

SR. LEO. You just never know what the Almighty has planned.

SR. HUBERT. Today, the Mistress of Novices, tomorrow—

SR. LEO. (*interrupting*) Tomorrow, the world could be saluting the first "nun ballerina!"

REV. MOTHER. (*to SR. LEO very patronizingly*) Of course, dear. (*to audience*) The important thing is that we can send those last four sisters off to claim their heavenly reward.

AUTHOR'S NOTE: In the Original New York Production, SR. HUBERT sang the lead in "HOLIER THAN THOU." In some subsequent productions the characters giving the next three speeches were reversed, and REV. MOTHER sang the lead in "HOLIER THAN THOU." Either version is permissible.

REV. MOTHER. And we can get back to concentrating on our *own* heavenly rewards. Because, after all, each and every one of us here tonight has the potential to become a saint!

SR. HUBERT. And you know something?

REV. MOTHER. What?

[MUSIC CUE 30: "HOLIER THAN THOU"]

SR. HUBERT.
IT'S NOT THAT HARD TO BE A SAINT.
ALL YOU HAVE TO DO
IS PICK A SAINT TO EMULATE
WHO MOST EMBODIES YOU.

THEN FIGURE OUT WHAT MADE THAT SAINT
THE IDOL OF TODAY.
THEN FOLLOW IN THOSE FOOTSTEPS
AND YOU'LL EARN THE RIGHT TO SAY:

I'M HOLIER THAN THOU.
I'VE GOT THE SPIRIT NOW.
I FEEL LIKE I'M IN HEAVEN
CAUSE I'M HOLIER THAN THOU.

I'M HOLIER THAN THOU.

I'VE GOT THE SPIRIT NOW.
I THANK GOD ALMIGHTY
THAT I'M HOLIER THAN THOU.
Alright! See how easy it is? Somebody, pick a saint!
  Sr. Amnesia. Saint Bernadette!
  Sr. Hubert. That's an excellent choice, Sister.
BERNADETTE OF LOURDES
CAN BE EASILY ACHIEVED.
SHE SAID SHE SAW A VIRGIN,
WHICH, OF COURSE, NO ONE BELIEVED.

PEOPLE SAID SHE'D LOST HER MIND,
THERE WAS NO LADY THERE.
SO GO AND FIND A VIRGIN
THEN COME BACK HERE AND DECLARE:

I'M HOLIER THAN THOU.
I'VE GOT THE SPIRIT NOW.
I FEEL LIKE I'M IN HEAVEN
CAUSE I'M HOLIER THAN THOU.

I'M HOLIER THAN THOU.
I'VE GOT THE SPIRIT NOW.
I THANK GOD ALMIGHTY
THAT I'M HOLIER THAN THOU.

(*to the other SISTERS*) Sisters, can you help me out?
  All but Sr. Hubert.
OOH, OOH, OOH. OOH, OOH, OOH.
OOH, OOH, OOH. OOH, OOH, OOH.
  Sr. Hubert. Oh, that's it! Thank-you. Let's have another.
  Sr. Robert Anne. Saint Lucy!
  Sr. Hubert.
LUCY WAS A VIRGIN
SO IF THAT TEST YOU DON'T FAIL.
LUCY COULD BE PERFECT
EXCEPT FOR ONE DETAIL.

LUCY WAS A MARTYR
WHICH COULD BE A BIT SEVERE.
  Rev. Mother.
I'LL GLADLY HELP HER OUT
AND POSTHUMOUSLY WE'LL HEAR:

I'M HOLIER THAN THOU.

SR. HUBERT. Give testimony, Sister.

REV. MOTHER.

I'VE GOT THE SPIRIT NOW.

I FEEL LIKE I'M IN HEAVEN

CAUSE I'M HOLIER THAN THOU.

SR. HUBERT and REV. MOTHER.

I'M HOLIER THAN THOU.

I'VE GOT THE SPIRIT NOW.

I THANK GOD ALMIGHTY

THAT I'M HOLIER THAN THOU.

ALL but SR. HUBERT.

OOH, OOH, OOH. OOH, OOH, OOH.

OOH, OOH, OOH. OOH, OOH, OOH.

SR. HUBERT. Alright, good people. There's something else I want to tell you!

YOU CAN BE SAINT ANTHONY

AND RUN A "LOST AND FOUND."

IF YOU'RE INTO TORTURE,

SAINT AGNES WAS RENOWNED.

MARY MAGDALEN IS PERFECT

FOR THE HOOKER WITH A DREAM.

WITH GOD ALL THINGS ARE POSSIBLE,

NOTHING'S TOO EXTREME!

ALL but SR. HUBERT.

I'M HOLIER THAN THOU.

I'M HOLIER THAN THOU.

I'M HOLIER THAN THOU.

I'M HOLIER THAN THOU.

(*Back-up singing continues. . . .*)

SR. HUBERT. Listen to me, now. When you leave here tonight, we want you to go home and pick a saint, so that you can get dowwwwn, to get uuuup, and get out on that road to heaven! Now, will you all put your hands together. (*She starts clapping in rhythm.*) Can I get an "Amen!"

ALL but SR. HUBERT. Amen!

SR. HUBERT. Amen!

ALL but SR. HUBERT. Amen!

SR. HUBERT. A-A-men!

ALL but SR. HUBERT. A-A-men!

SR. HUBERT. A-A-men!

ALL but SR. HUBERT. A-A-men!

ALL.

I'M HOLIER THAN THOU.
I'VE GOT THE SPIRIT NOW.
I FEEL LIKE I'M IN HEAVEN
CAUSE I'M HOLIER THAN THOU.

I'M HOLIER THAN THOU.
I'VE GOT THE SPIRIT NOW.
I THANK GOD ALMIGHTY
THAT I'M HOLIER THAN THOU.

SR. HUBERT. One more time!

ALL.

I'M HOLIER THAN THOU.
I'VE GOT THE SPIRIT NOW.
I FEEL LIKE I'M IN HEAVEN
CAUSE I'M HOLIER THAN THOU.

I'M HOLIER THAN THOU.
I'VE GOT THE SPIRIT NOOOOOOOOWWWW!

SR. HUBERT.

I FEEL LIKE I'M IN HEAVEN—

*(She improvises some gospel riffs as we hear the others shouting
such things as, "Sing it, Sister," "Praise the lord," etc.)*

I SAID, I FEEL LIKE I'M IN HEAVEN.

SR. ROBERT ANNE. Why, Sister, why?

SR. HUBERT. Because—

ALL but SR. HUBERT. Why?

SR. HUBERT. Because—

ALL but SR. HUBERT. Why?

SR. HUBERT.

BECAUSE, I AM HOLIER
THAAAAAAAAANNN

SR. HUBERT.	ALL but SR. HUBERT.
THOU!	I'M HOLIER THAN THOU!
	I'M HOLIER THAN THOU!
	I'M HOLIER THAN THOU!

ALL.

HOLIER THAN THOU! YOW!

[MUSIC CUE 31: NUNSENSE REPRISE]

"NUNSENSE REPRISE"

ALL.
NUNSENSE IS HABIT-FORMING
THAT'S WHAT PEOPLE SAY.
WE'RE HERE TO PROVE THAT NUNS ARE FUN,
PERHAPS A BIT RISQUE.

WE STILL WEAR OUR HABITS
TO RETAIN OUR MAGIC SPELL.
AND THOUGH WE'RE ON OUR WAY TO HEAVEN,
WE'RE HERE TO RAISE SOME HELL!
　　CONDUCTOR. Sell it, Girls!
　　ALL.
TURN UP THE SPOTLIGHT,
CAUSE WHEN WE GOT LIGHT
ALL THAT WE CAN SAY
IS, "IT REALLY HAS BEEN FUN.
THANK-YOU EACH AND EVERYONE."
IT'S TIME TO END OUR PLAY!
BY THE WAY, GOD BLESS YOU EACH DAY!

[MUSIC CUE 32: BOWS AND EXIT MUSIC]

End ACT TWO

COSTUME PLOT

All five actresses wear the habit of "The Little Sisters of Hoboken" consisting of:

Black tights
Black long sleeve T-shirt
Black orthopedic oxford shoes
Black tunic with breast pocket
Black belt buckled in the back
Fifteen decade rosary hung from the left side of the belt
Black scapular
White guimpe (bib collar)
White wimple (headpiece)
Black veil lined with white*

The Reverend Mother wears a crucifix that hangs just below the guimpe (bib collar). The cord on the crucifix goes under the guimpe.

If glasses are worn to give added character to any of the nuns, they should be of plain design, with the "arms" worn inside the wimple.

Any additional "costume" pieces are listed under "props."

---

*The novice, SISTER MARY LEO, wears an all-white veil.

SET PROPS

PROP	LOCATION
Statues of Mary and Joseph	Either side of the proscenium
Flag on floor stand	Next to statue of St. Joseph
"Grease" logo	Hung upstage
Basketball hoops (optional)	Hung on either side of the stage or in the auditorium
Basketball	Placed randomly on stage floor
School Bell (electric)	Mounted on upstage wall
Movie screen	Mounted in arch over platform (A portable screen is optional.)
Juke box or record player	Upstage right
Two large posters (Elvis, James Dean, Sandra Dee)	Hung near juke box
Small stool	Next to juke box
Lunch counter on rolling platform with 3 or 4 stools and hidden shelf in back	Downstage right
Cake plate with top and prop cake, salt, pepper, etc.	On lunch counter top
Three aprons (costume)	Preset on shelf behind lunch counter
Easel with poster announcing Little Sisters of Hoboken Benefit	Center stage
Black "skirt" with two velcro tabs on top corners	Draped around base of easel
Car seat with solid back painted like the rear of	Upstage center

a 1950's car, on rolling
platform

Three hair dryers	Mounted upstage on wall over car seat
Exercycle	Upstage left
Bed with spread and pillows	Downstage left
Marilyn Monroe poster (posed in swimsuit, with velcro tabs at waist used for attaching skirt which is preset on base of easel)	Hung upstage left
Set of lockers	On platform
Wall phone or pay phone	Mounted on platform wall
Water cooler	On platform
Carousel projector with slides	Rear of theatre

HAND PROPS
(Listed according to location and actress)

Stage Left:

Quiz questions on 3 × 5 cards (SR. AMNESIA)
Prizes (2 per performance) (SR. AMNESIA)
Bathrobe (SR. LEO)
Toe shoes (SR. LEO)
Fuzzy slippers (SR. LEO)
Paper cup (SR. ROBERT ANNE)
Lilacs with gift card (SR. LEO)
Small paper bag with "RUSH" bottle inside (SR. ROBERT ANNE)
Chef's hat (SR. ROBERT ANNE)
Automatic Umbrella (REV. MOTHER)
Soup tureen with ladle (SR. ROBERT ANNE)
"Dying Nun" hat (SR. LEO)

Stage Right:

"Sister Mary Annette" puppet (SR. AMNESIA)
Plastic fruit hung on wire headband (SR. ROBERT ANNE)
Small booklet entitled "The Understudy" (SR. ROBERT ANNE)
Maracas (SR. ROBERT ANNE)
Shopping bag with four pair of tap shoes (SR. HUBERT)
Summons from New Jersey Board of Health (REV. MOTHER)
"Baking with the B.V.M." cookbook (SR. AMNESIA)
Mixing bowl (SR. AMNESIA)
Whisk (SR. AMNESIA)
Wooden spoon (SR. AMNESIA)
Egg carton (SR. AMNESIA)
Homemade crooked wooden bookstand (SR. AMNESIA)

In Locker on Platform:

Wooden ruler on ring (SR. AMNESIA)

In Appropriate Dressing Rooms:

Frog clicker (REV. MOTHER)
Keys on leather strap (SR. ROBERT ANNE)
Belt clip to hold ruler (SR. AMNESIA)
Four wedding bands (REV. MOTHER, SR. ROBERT ANNE, SR. HUBERT and SR. AMNESIA)

e Playbill for the original production of *Nunsense* had an un-
ual format for its cast's "bios," and local producers may adapt
ese to suit their needs:

Who's Who in the Cast

STER MARY REGINA, the beloved Mother Superior of the
ttle Sisters of Hoboken, is originally from a small county in
eland called Kilquirky. She headed the pioneering group of re-
ious who established the leper colony in the Mediterranean
d later returned to Hoboken as Superior General of the Order.
ter *Nunsense*, Mother Superior says she has no desire to con-
ue in the theatre. But rumor has it that she would consider do-
g national commercials or a television series to raise money for
e Order. Prior to taking her vows, Sister Mary Regina was
ctress' Name). (Actress' credits.)

STER MARY HUBERT entered the Little Sisters of Hoboken
on graduation from Precious Blood Elementary School. Sis-
: currently serves the Order as Mistress of Novices, training
w recruits. Her position is not unlike a drill sergeant, however,
e is the first to point out that her approach is more gentle—
t firm. Sister is a little "off-the-wall" at times but this has been
tributed to the fact that she was trampled by a camel that went
serk during the annual nativity pageant held in the leper col-
y. (She was portraying one of the three wise men.) Sister Mary
ubert is the former (Actress' Name). Miss (Name) was seen
. (list credits.)

STER MARY ROBERT ANNE was a child of a disadvan-
ged Brooklyn family. After dropping out of Verna's Cashier
hool, Reverend Mother took pity on poor little (Actress'
ame) and accepted her into the Little Sisters of Hoboken,
here she became Sister Mary Robert Anne. Today she is one of
e most popular sisters with New Jersey kids because she speaks
eir language. Reverend Mother regrets the fact that a lot of
is language is unprintable. Sister Robert Anne had a very
eckered career prior to entering the convent, including acting
ints in (Actress' credits). The nuns rarely discuss (Name's) (ie.
year-old son).

STER MARY AMNESIA is truly a lost soul. She arrived at

79

the convent in her habit without a clue as to her identity . . .
calling only that a crucifix fell on her head. It has been said th
she resembles (Actress' Name), who learned ventriloquism wh
she became a Little Sister of Hoboken and previously (cre
its . . .).

SISTER MARY LEO came to the order from an Illinois far
She entered the convent to dedicate her life to God through t
dance. Many people think that she took her name from t
famous "leotard," but that is not true. She is named after h
Uncle Leo, a notorious Chicago gangster. Sister thought that
taking his name, the Lord would go easy on him. She is a novi
and has much to learn. Before joining the Order, Sister w
known as (Actress' Name), who tested her dancing ability by a
pearing in (credits . . .). Prior to taking her vow of poverty, S
ter supported herself by portraying (more credits . . .).

DAN GOGGIN (*Writer*) conceived the idea for the music
Nunsense after the phenomenal success of the Nunsense greeti
card line, which he created with Marilyn Farina. Dan has al
written scores for the Off-Broadway musical *Hark*; the Broa
way production *Legend*, starring Elizabeth Ashley and F. Murra
Abraham; *Seven*, starring Jane White; the musical *A One-W*
Ticket to Broadway; and two revues: *Because We're Decade*
and *Something for Everybody's Mother*. Dan has applied for a
mission to the Little Order of Hoboken, but Sister Mary Regi
says she is much too busy with *Nunsense* to answer any lette
now.

DIRECTOR'S NAME (*Director*) was released from his vows
Brother Futon Fouette. This occurred after the Bishop di
covered that Brother Futon had used his habit as a parachute
jump from a jetliner onto a burning building, where he singl
handedly saved 300 pounds of uncut cocaine from the flame
giving rise to his favorite expression: "Come fly with me!" Sin
then, as (Director's Name), he has (credits . . .).

BROTHER (NAME) (*Musical Director*) is our convent m
sician. He was part of the original contingent who establishe
the leper colony served by the Order. Brother achieved muc
notoriety when he published his first music book, *Two Part In*
ventions for the Fingerless, which he dedicated to the leper